The
Great
Wedding

THE GREAT WEDDING

Max Evans

with an introduction by
John Sinor

UNIVERSITY OF NEW MEXICO PRESS

Albuquerque

Library of Congress Cataloging in Publication Data

Evans, Max.
  The great wedding.

  Previously published in anthology entitled: Three short novels.
  I. Title.
PS3555.V23G7   1983   813'.54   83-10214
ISBN 0-8263-0701-9 (pbk.)

Manufactured in the United States of America.
Library of Congress Catalog Card Number 83-10214.
International Standard Book Number 0-8263-0701-9.

Introduction

This little book you are holding in your hands almost got itself lost. Up to now it had one printing, in a collection that included two other Max Evans stories. The other two became something akin to classics.

One of the other tales was "The One-Eyed Sky," a raw story of the Texas plains in which Evans sucks his readers right inside the minds of a couple of valiant mothers using every instinct they possess to protect their young. The marvel of the work is that one mother is an aging cow during and just after the birth of her last calf, and the other is a coyote trying to find food for her hungry pups.

The other story was "My Partner," the saga of a survival journey by an old man and a boy of twelve that I think Mark Twain would have been pleased to have written.

But in a way *The Great Wedding* should have been at least the second most successful of all Max Evans's books. The biggest one for him, naturally, was *The Rounders*. It hit the best-seller lists and was turned into a bright motion picture comedy starring Henry Fonda and Glenn Ford. Later it even became a television series for a while.

The Rounders concerned the misadventures of two contemporary cowboys and one contemporary cow pony, all three with about the same IQ. Dusty and Wrangler and the horse, Old Fooler, charge through life in about twelve different directions at the same time, trying to cram years of good healthy lust, whiskey, gambling, exuberance, and general disturbance of the peace into every payday.

The Great Wedding is the sequel to *The Rounders,* featuring the same insane trio.

Not many writers are willing to take a shot at putting down on paper a definition of humor, but I have an idea of what a lot of it is: Humor is something bad happening to somebody else. I don't mean something terrible and violent. I'm just talking about general bad news that could have happened to us. There's nothing really funny about getting hit in the face with a pie—unless it happens to somebody else. There's not a blessed thing funny about being kicked by a horse—unless we read about it happening to somebody we would like to have kicked by a horse. There's nothing funny about shoveling millions of shovels of manure—unless it is being done by an ignorant cowboy as a part of another ignorant cowboy's plan to get his partner to get so sick of cowboying that he becomes willing to commit that most desperate act of all—marriage—but marriage to a woman rich enough to take care of both of them in style the rest of their lives so their saddle sores and aching bones can finally heal.

Max Evans understands this kind of humor as well as anybody I know. And in Dusty and Wrangler he has created two of the sorriest, most pitiful heroes this side of Don Quixote and Sancho Panza. If they weren't so hilarious in their wild misadventures, you would cry for them.

I've known Max for a good many years now and from time to time we have even done some of the same dumb things he has Dusty and Wrangler do. Max, who started cowboying just before his twelfth birthday, knows the people he writes about as well as he knows the scars on his knuckles and the weather reports in his formerly broken bones.

Max might still be a busted-up cowboy if he hadn't gotten his hands on some of his boss's books in the bunkhouse. From cowboying and reading, he drifted into painting and mining. In his mining investments he got into drifts well over his head. The only solution he could see to crawling out from under an $85,000 pile of debts was to sit down and write himself a best-selling novel. Why not? He had read a few books.

The incredible thing was that he did just that. And *The Rounders* was born. The filming of that got him into the motion picture business, and soon he was writing screenplays, doctoring screenplays, and writing more books and short stories. He has even directed, produced, and acted in films. (Next time you watch *The Ballad of Cable Hogue* on television look for the surly old shotgun rider beside Slim Pickens on the stagecoach. That's Max.)

Several producers have tried to get *The Great Wedding* in front of the cameras, and maybe someday it will get done. The problem, so far, has been the screenplay. What the characters do is funny, all right, but not nearly as funny as Max, narrating the story as Dusty, tells it. And the narration, or voice-over, technique is considered old hat these days by a lot of the people who have their hands on the production cash in Hollywood.

Still, producers keep taking options on the book and sending checks every once in a while to Max. And, borrowing words back from Wrangler, Max says, "That just tickles me plumb to death."

In the meantime the University of New Mexico Press has had the foresight to reprint this and several other of Max's books.

That's an idea as bright as the New Mexico sunshine.

San Diego, California   JOHN SINOR

THE GREAT WEDDING

One

HE WAS at it again. Jim Ed Love was smooth-talking hell out of me and poor old Wrangler.

"Now, boys, I had a tough time gettin' you fellers out of that Hi Lo jail. Why you was charged with everything but rape, and if I hadn't seen the kind of gals you was courtin' I'da figured you guilty of that . . . drunk, disturbin' the peace, assaulting an officer of the law . . ." Then he rubbed his great big whey belly shaking that gold watch chain and said, like he was talking to a couple of runny-nose orphans, "Tch, tch."

I knew we were trapped. Everything he said was true and then some. He had picked up a bunch of hot checks and fixed it with the judge to get us sprung.

I looked down at little, squatty Wrangler where he stood on his bent-out legs picking his nose. Right at this minute I was wishing so hard my corns ached that old Wrangler was married to a rich woman, but it was head-hurting clear that getting him married was not going to be the easiest job I ever had. Like the town fellers say, "Where there's a will . . ." and it was the only way I could figure out to get away from Jim Ed and get me a decent job for once in my life.

Jim Ed interrupted my thinking with, "Now, fellers, I know you had a reasonably hard winter down at the lower camp, what with spending the whole year gatherin' wild cows and such. I know you missed out on a lot of fun around the ranch here — poker games in the bunkhouse, drinkin' bouts ever' other Saturday in Hi Lo. Well, that ain't goin' to be no more."

I was beginning to believe him till he started rubbing that sirloin-manufactured belly and caressing the brim of that cloud-white fifty-dollar hat.

"No siree, fellers — " He laid one diamond-covered hand out on my shoulder so heavy and friendly if I'd had a tail I'd have wagged it hairless. "No siree, you're going to stay within a day's ride of headquarters where you can be in on *everything*. Now, we're startin' the roundup in a few weeks. You boys know that's the highlight of the year — sort of the sugar in the coffee so to speak."

Well, guess what? That is right, we shook hands and agreed to stay on at the slave-driving JL Ranch. We walked out of the house feeling kind of numb. There in the back of the pickup was Old Fooler.

I said, "Wrangler, at least this'll give me a chance to get even with that good-for-nothing-but-trouble horse on my own terms. I don't mind the fact that he's tried to kill me ever' way known to horse, man and maybe God, but when he jumped the rail and lost us all that money in the horse race at Hi Lo, well, the right words are goin' beggin'."

Wrangler grunted out of his somewhat caved-in face and Old Fooler seemed to actually smile at me. It caused another one of them uneasy feelings, that smile. If he'd showed his teeth I would have known what to do — take a fence post and bust him between the ears.

As usual Jim Ed had a big, heavy calf crop that spring and all the other ranchers sent "reps" over for the fall roundup to see if any of their cattle were mixed in with the JL brand. There wasn't much time for visiting among old friends. Jim Ed saw to that. I will say one thing, he gave me and Wrangler the great honor of assigning us the outside circle. Now that is the longest and hardest ride and takes the best cowboys to handle it. I don't think that had much to do with what kind of cowboys we were but more to do with the long, hard ride.

They had a Dodge Power Wagon all rigged up like an old-time chuck wagon with a chuck box on the back and a cranky cook up front. Roundup was like Jim Ed said, "sugar in the coffee."

I mounted Old Fooler for the first circle and Wrangler roped him a brown out of the remuda. We worked up through the brush making a wide circle, jumping out little bunches of cattle now and then. We shoved them back down to the holding grounds on the flats. Old Fooler was working smooth and right. A cow no sooner tried to turn back than that old devil blue roan was biting her right in the rump.

By noon the horses were tiring so we rode back down to the remuda and roped two fresh mounts. I knew tomorrow we'd be working in rougher country and I wanted that crazy Fooler horse under me.

We rode back out for the brush under a sure enough blue sky. The grass on Jim Ed's outfit looked riper than yellow corn and thicker than hair on a skunk's tail. It was what is known among some thoughtful folks as a mighty fine fall day.

We reined up to roll ourselves a smoke and I said, "Wrangler, there comes a time in every cowboy's life when he needs to hang up his spurs for a spell. Sort of set in the saddle without movin', so to speak," and I gazed off into about nine hundred miles of space.

Wrangler grunted in what sounded to me like drunk Navaho and took a drag on his smoke that made her burn halfway to his jaws right before my eyes.

"Now for us old, broke-up cowboys they ain't too many choices."

He looked at me, those little rat-shaped eyes just asking "How?" right out loud.

"First, we can't draw none of this here unemployment pay. Cowboys ain't never had any of that. Second, it's mighty hard and costly to get insurance on a cowboy. So collecting that is next to impossible. Now we could go on relief. You know, get hungry enough a feller'll do anything."

"Oh, it's against the law to starve to death in this country," said Wrangler.

"How do you figger that?"

"Well, if you get so hungry and weak you cain't stand up, some damn fool will drag you in off the street and feed you."

This last, one of the longest speeches in history made by Wrangler, kinda defeated my purpose so I whipped up and got to the main point.

"Course a man could save all that embarrassment and injury to his pride by marrying a rich woman."

"That ain't easy," Wrangler said with great wisdom.

"Ain't nothin' easy," I said battling right back. "Besides a feller could do a lot of good in the world, like takin' care of his old bunged-up friends by givin' them good jobs on an easy-to-run outfit."

"Well, why don't you marry one?" said that dumb Wrangler.

I swallered hard and studied that nine hundred miles of space again, then I said, "I just ain't got the charm, that's all. If I had what you have, Wrangler, I'd of been hooked up years ago."

He sort of stiffened in the saddle and I could tell this last had taken hold. Course, if a man had to admit to who was the best looking between us, old Wrangler wouldn't even be sucking hind teat, he'd be dragging right by the end of the tail. But I figured it best to keep him thinking the other way.

Two

I DID some hard thinking. If I was going to get Wrangler married off the best thing to do was discourage him towards punching cows every way I could. So to start with, I make the widest circle that day I ever heard of. A cowboy may have a rawhide hind-end, but that won't keep it from getting numb.

That evening we finished filling up on beans and biscuits just as the sun turned off. Most of the boys hit their bedrolls early. Old Wrangler didn't even say goodnight.

The cook was cleaning up and the boys riding night herd out in the flats were wishing they were back in camp. I eased back on my bedroll and tried to think some more. I stared up at those zillion stars, nothing helped. It's pretty hard to think with a numb ass.

The next day we caught up our horses. Wrangler's had a hump in his back like a snake-bit hog. He saddled him, led him up a few steps and climbed on. The brown broke out in a dead run, swallered his head and went straight up about six feet. When he came down he hit the ground with all four feet bunched close together. I felt like my neck was broken just watching, but it didn't even seem to bother Wrangler because he just headed him off in the direction we were going to work.

I mounted up and followed. But just before I did, I grabbed a bottle of Hi-Life the cook used to get rid of stray dogs, and shoved it in my chaps pocket. By the time I caught Wrangler he had pulled the bronc's head up where it belongs.

"Feels good, don't he?"

Wrangler grunted.

We rode on a piece before the horse settled down enough so Wrangler would tear his hand away from the saddle horn.

"This here is some life, ain't it, Wrangler? Get up in the morning with nothing but smoke in your eyes to warm by. The coffee's so thick and bitter it tastes like cedar bark. The biscuits harder'n cinch rings and the bacon is salty and tooth-breakin' tough. Nice gentle horses, too. Easy on a man's old broken bones. You know what I heard the last time we were in Hi Lo?"

Grunt.

"Well, I heard that ever' time an old boy rode a bucking horse it meant one less drunk he could go on!"

He twisted his head around on his shoulders, staring with his eyes wide open. He didn't say anything but I could tell I'd penetrated to the quick.

The sun was up and shining on the mesas and we could see a few fresh tracks now. We reined up.

"Look," I said, pointing way off to the west, "ain't that

a bunch of cattle in that opening between them rock bluffs?"

He looked.

I slipped the Hi-Life out and poured it right plentifully on the root of his horse's tail. Now when you pour this stuff on a dog it soaks down around the hair roots and he will run a mile in two minutes, yapping his head off — and he won't be back to visit. It has a funny smell, something like chloroform, so I thought I'd talk fast and keep Wrangler's mind clean off this horse's intentions.

"Do you see 'em?"

"Naw."

"You sure?"

"Yaw."

Blooey! Away they went. Two jumps out and one back. Wrangler went east and the old pony south.

I took off after the horse feeling mighty sorry about Wrangler having to walk. I just wasn't going to let that happen to my best friend. Way up on the mesa I could hear brush popping and hoofs pounding against rock. It took me quite a spell to hem the brown up in a blind draw and catch him. Then I rode out in a patch of brush where I could look back down at Wrangler. He was up limping around, twisting his head one way and another trying to hear my return.

I sat there about an hour, real still, feeling it my duty to let Wrangler have a chance to get over his embarrassment.

When I finally rode up and said, "Feels good, don't he?" I thought Wrangler was going to choke on all the cuss words he was spitting out.

We finally moved several little bunches of cattle down towards the main herd.

It had been a hard day but nothing like the night. Breakfast came just after midnight it seemed to me. Old Wrangler was sure limping. Of course, he's not much of a walker at his best.

We rode out about a mile from camp when I got itchy to go on with my plans. But I was afraid to pull the cattle-spotting stunt again. Pretty soon old Wrangler pulled it for me. He thought he'd located some stock.

"Yeah," I said, "I believe that is a couple of head, but what is that spot off about fifty yards to the right?" Then I poured on the Hi-Life.

Before it could soak in, old Wrangler spurred up a couple of steps, yanked back on the reins and jumped off. Their heads went down together as Wrangler bit down on the horse's ear. That ole pony was shaking all over trying to make up his mind which end was hurting the most. Wrangler just held him there with his ear clinched between his teeth. After a while Wrangler turned loose and the Hi-Life effects must have been gone because the horse just kind of scooted around, snorted at Wrangler a couple of times and settled down.

I said, "What'n hell's the matter?"

"I ain't sure," he said, "but this ole pony smelled just like that one did yesterday."

We rode back to camp late that afternoon with me and Wrangler feeling just about the same, sort of let-down and mean as bloody-nosed bears.

We finished the roundup and all I could say when they hauled all those fat, profitable calves off to market in those big long red cattle trucks was, "It sure would be nice if those were yours, Wrangler. Just think, you could go on up to Denver with 'em and stay drunk all the time you was countin' your money."

"They ain't mine," he said.

I had to agree.

Three

OLD JIM ED sure hadn't lied to us. We could play poker any night we wanted with the boys in the bunkhouse. The trouble was, our hands were so bent and sore from lifting bales of hay we couldn't shuffle the cards.

Haying was a big thing on the JL. South of the house were acres and acres of hayfields, all irrigated from springs. Jim Ed always kept a lot of extra hay so he'd have it ready in case of a big blizzard. I'd heard that one winter he'd come into thousands of acres in Texas and Colorado by controlling the feed market, and made a fortune selling hay to stricken ranchers. Nice feller, our boss.

I really caught Jim Ed off guard when I volunteered mine and Wrangler's services for this hay gathering. Of course, Wrangler didn't know this and I decided it wasn't my place to tell him.

Now this hay was cut and crushed into bales weighing about eighty pounds apiece and there were thousands of them. We pitched bales all day long onto a flatbed truck, then we piled one on top of the other into a pyramid-shaped stack. This was just the first cutting. There'd be another for us later.

"Wrangler," I said, stopping to take a breath and a smoke, "if a man was married to a rich woman he wouldn't have to put up hay. As far as that goes his number one foreman wouldn't either."

"How come?"

"Why, we'd either hire it done or buy it from some other fool. A man needs to be in shape to rodeo and go dancin'. He shouldn't be gettin' out of trainin' by crackin' his back on this hay."

"Sounds fine," he said.

I was encouraged by his enthusiasm.

"Now soon as we get a couple of paydays together, I think we ought to go in and see Rosie at the General Mercantile. It's been two years since her old man died. She must be gettin' lonesome for some male company."

Grunt.

"Now think of this, Wrangler, she's got a big store paid for, a twenty-section ranch running along the main highway with plenty of improvements and water, and no tellin' what else."

"She ain't gonna marry no cowboy."

I hadn't thought about this part of it. It was true that Rosie had known at least three thousand broken-down, worthless cowboys in her time. We'd just have to figure a way to make old Wrangler appear different. I had plenty of time to think about it the next few days.

We put up the hay and I told Jim Ed on the sly that I felt me and Wrangler had had it too soft and wondered if he couldn't find us a fence-building job. He did the next morning.

One of his big springs had turned into a bog. Cows were commencing to get out in it and sink down so far they had to be roped and pulled out. It would take a strong fence to enclose it.

Now a posthole digger is a mighty mean-looking thing to get hold of just standing still, but when you raise the handles as high as you can reach and drive it into the hard ground all day long, it is something most cowboys won't even think of, much less talk about. After the holes are dug, the posts have to be lined up straight and tapped into the ground solid. Then you stretch the wire and staple it to the posts. On top of all that you build gates and hang deadmen (rocks tied to the corner post and buried in the ground) so it will stand upright.

It might be an interesting change of work for a rock-busting prisoner, but it was beginning to tell on us cowboys. This was what I wanted. I was willing to go through any sacrifice to show my friend the bright and sparkling righteousness of hooking up with a rich woman.

I said, "You got to admit that things would look better to us if you was roastin' your shins out at Rosie's ranchhouse knowin' that she was in town selling them beans and bacon, and your best friend was out in the pasture looking after your cattle. Why, right now instead of holding a bunch of blood blisters in both hands you could be caressin' a fat bottle of bourbon. Not only that but you could bed down tonight full of fine steak and whiskey right next to big-teated Rosie. As it is, you'll sleep in a cold bunkhouse full of cold, dirty cowboys."

"There's some difference there," Wrangler admitted.

Well I figured he was far enough along for me to make my real sales talk — the one I'd been studying over and saving up.

"Wrangler, if Old Fooler was a genuine gentle horse, one you could trust your life with . . ."

"Wouldn't even trust him with Jim Ed's life."

"I know, but what I mean, supposin' he *was* gentle."

"Yeah."

"Would you bet on him in a horse race against anything around Hi Lo?"

"Hell yes. Why?"

"I'll tell you why, because I've got a plan to make you look really right in Rosie's eyes. Not only that, but you'll appear to be the smartest cowboy this side of Canada."

"That's lots of country."

"You're a smart cowboy."

"How come?"

"Listen now, listen like you was goin' to be *given* a thousand dollars worth of Vince Moore's bootleg whiskey if you don't miss a word I say."

Four

I WAS STILL trying to explain things when we drove up in front of Vince Moore's house.

Now I'll say this for Vince's place: even if the windmill is generally broken, corral poles split and falling all over, panes out of half the windows, the chimney leaking smoke from a loose joint, the porch leaning way to the north, there is plenty of action — chickens scratching about and doing things all over the yard, dogs barking and wagging tails at the same time, dirty-faced kids peeking around the porch, the corner of the house, and between their mother's legs and Vince throwing the door to the outhouse open yelling, "Don't leave, boys. I'll finish in a breeze."

"Howdy, Mrs. Moore."

"What do you mean, 'Mrs. Moore'? Now, Dusty Jones, you know my name is Marthy."

"That I do, Marthy."

"Howdy, Marthy," said Wrangler.

"Why howdy, Wrangler Lewis," she said, pushing the straight cords of hair back behind her ears, and trying to shove her chest out and lift her suckling glands just a little. It was too late for that — round fifteen years too late. Kids just plain have a habit of swinging down on them instead of up, and when you've had as many kids as Marthy . . .

"Coffee?" she asked as we stepped inside, "Er . . . something else?"

"Something else sounds mighty fine to me," said Wrangler, suddenly snapping to.

She got some big tin cups from the cupboard, set them out in front of us and said Vince would be there in a minute to get the *goody* for us.

"What you boys been doin' besides Jim Ed's dirty work?"

"That's all, Marthy. That's all."

Wrangler nodded.

Jim Ed had been able to take over everybody's ranch that jogged into his but Vince's little outfit. He broke Vince as a cowman, but Vince had come on strong as a bootlegger — of course, strong to Vince might be weak to other people. If he had a new batch of whiskey made up, a half sack of beans and the same of flour he was pretty stable. Besides he liked chasing coyotes with his old skinny dogs better than he did cattle anyway.

Vince came busting through the door just knocking kids seven ways, shaking hands, pouring whiskey and talking like a radio all at once. He set the jug down on the table, threw a bunch of grease shaped like a hat on the floor and said, "It sure is good to see you. It sure is." Then his face sort of fogged over. He whammed his cup down and ran to the door. "I knew it," he yelled. "By god I knew it. The mean-eyed son of a bitch is still alive. You ain't tradin' him to me again! He tore up my corrals, fences, everything!" His hair had fallen down over his milky eyes but he was too mad to see anyway.

"Now calm down, Vince," I said. "Why, I wouldn't trade you that blazed-face roan for your whole outfit, kids and all."

Vince sorta whoa'd a minute, breathing like he had to and even if his eyes were covered I knew they were bugging.

"Liars, liars!" he said through clenched teeth as he glanced at Old Fooler standing peaceful-like in the back of the pickup. "I . . . I . . ."

"Now here, have another drink and listen to what we've thought up."

Vince's hair was kinda like Marthy's only thinner and rattier looking. I was glad when he pushed it out of his eyes so I could tell if it had come in his mind to grab the shotgun off the wall and blow my cockeyed head off.

"Here's the plan, Ever'body knows that Old Fooler can outrun anything in the country. He proved that last Fourth of July when he was leading the best horse around by four jumps."

"I tell you I wouldn't have that damn horse if you gave me Jim Ed's ranch to take him."

"Now, Vince, I ain't giving you no sales talk. Just listen." He poured us another drink while I went on, "At the same time ever'body knows that horse jumped the rail and had a runaway."

"We lost," said Wrangler.

"That's right, we lost," I agreed. "We lost ever'thing we'd won in the rodeo and a whole year's wages. Taking ever'thing into consideration I want to ask you boys a question."

"Shoot."

Wrangler said, "Uh."

"Will you fellers agree that you can depend on Old Fooler to mess up no matter what?"

"Hooray, hell yes, and I should say so right out loud in church," said Vince.

"Ever' goddamned time," said Wrangler.

"That's all I need to know," I said, smiling into my cup. "Now, I'm goin' to wind this up fast, so hang on and listen close."

Vince leaned forward across the table. Wrangler humped up with his cup stopped dead-still an inch from his mouth. That's listening, brother.

"Well, if Old Fooler was to suddenly turn black . . ."

"Oh good! You're goin' to kill him and let him rot," Vince said hopefully.

"Will you fellers let me do the talking. Now if he was to turn black on the outside . . . say that somebody rubbed some of that charcoal you use all the time to make this wonderful stuff we're drinkin' all over that roan, he'd turn black wouldn't he?"

"Blacker'n a bear's butt," said Wrangler snapping to a little more all the time.

"Blacker'n Jim Ed's heart," said Vince.

"Now, don't get carried away," said Marthy from over in the corner where she was patching a shirt.

"Now, if some folks around Hi Lo was to see this here beautiful black horse at a distance — just see him runnin' loose and free they would know he was a runnin' fool. Right?"

"Right."

"Right."

"All right, then. In that case if somebody was to match a race on that little bay of yours, Vince, then ever'body would bet on the black."

"Right, by god."

"Whoopeee," Wrangler agreed strongly.

I stopped for breath and poured us all another cup of that perfect thirst quencher from the crock jug.

"If we was to have five hundred dollars bet on the bay we would be sure to win, huh?"

"Couldn't miss," said Vince, "because that Old Fooler horse would jump the rail, fall down, start bucking or running the wrong way before you'd get a quarter of the way around the track."

"Well, me and Wrangler here ain't been to town, Vince, in several paydays, and we've got her right here in cash!" I threw it all out on the table, and Vince tried to swaller the tin cup.

"Now all you got to do is co-operate a little and we'll clean out that Hi Lo so fast it won't know what county it's in."

On the way over to Vince's I told Wrangler that if we'd

tip Rosie off so she'd get down some good fat bets, she would sure appreciate the winnings. Not only that, but she'd just bust her big, fat drawers wanting to marry old Wrangler when I told her it was *all* his idea. A smart man like that is hard to find.

Vince stood up and sloshed out another round.

"Dusty, you're a go-gettin' son of a bitch!"

"Wrangler," I asked, feeling kind of embarrassed at all that praise, "what do you think?"

"Whatever suits you just tickles me plumb to death."

I knew from past experiences I had Wrangler sold to the gut hollow.

Five

WE GOT Old Fooler out of the pickup. It wasn't easy to do, but with the help of Vince's jug we got her done. Vince brought out a keg of charcoal and we started rubbing it on him.

"Ain't that purty?" I said.

"Yeah," said Wrangler.

"It ain't gonna stay put, fellers," said Vince.

"It don't have to stay long," I said.

"Just long enough to clean out Hi Lo," said Wrangler.

Right there, I, Dusty Jones, started using this head of mine for smart purposes again. I never felt so cockeyed smart in my whole life.

"Vince?"

"Yeah, Dusty."

"You got any varnish?"

"Sure have, by doggies, a whole gallon of it. Had it for years. Been aimin' to use it on somethin' like the floor or maybe a wagon bed."

"Your problems are over."

"How's that?"

"Just get it, Vince. Just bring it to old Dusty."

While Vince went to get the varnish I went back in the house to see Marthy on important business.

"Marthy, do you have a fly sprayer?"

"Yeah, but we ain't had any ammunition for it in three years. Flies ain't bad out here anyway, not enough fer 'em to eat."

"Well, let me borrow it for just a spell."

She handed it over.

"Now, boys, watch this," I said as I poured the varnish in the flysprayer. They sure did watch.

Then I reared back and mashed the handle with the machine aimed right at Old Fooler. Nothing happened. I tried her again. The same.

"It's too thick," I said, and grabbed the jug away from Wrangler. He put up quite a fight till I explained I was only going to use a shot or two.

I poured half the varnish out of the spray and filled it up with whiskey. Then I gave her a good shaking and mashed that handle again. The trick was done. That stuff sprayed out of there and settled the charcoal down just like it had grown that way.

"By god, fellers," old Vince said, "I done said it, that Dusty's a go-gettin' son of a bitch!"

I didn't even have time to agree. I said, "Get your bay horse, Vince, we're headin' for Hi Lo."

Wrangler said, "Whoooooopeee and hurrah," and jumped just as high as he could right straight up in the air. At that he just barely got off the ground.

We crowded both horses in the pickup bed, Vince fetched another jug and we all yelled goodbye at Marthy and the kids. When they answered back it sounded like a jail full of drunks. Away we went.

Just before getting into Hi Lo we turned off down a little wagon road and hunted some brush. We unloaded the horses. I tied Old Fooler with a double catch-rope to a stout cedar.

"Now, Vince, give me and old Wrangler about an hour in town. Then you come ridin' in like you hadn't seen us in a year. You know what to do from there on."

"Sure do," he said. "Here, fellers, give me that jug. It's gonna get lonesome out here the next hour."

When times were better, Hi Lo had several saloons. Now there were just two, the Double Duty and the Wildcat. It didn't take a man long to make up his mind. Today we picked Nick Barnes' Wildcat.

"Well, looky here," he said, "if it ain't Dusty and Wrangler. Ain't seen you boys since the Fourth of July."

"We ain't been anywhere to be seen," I said.

"Whiskey," Wrangler said.

"Whiskey," I said.

"Comin' up. Doubles or singles?"

"One of each," I said.

"Too bad the way that old roan horse double-crossed you in that race, Dusty. You boys could have bought old Jim Ed's whole outfit with those winnings."

"Well, I ain't aimin' to lose another." I wanted to thank Nick for bringing up the right subject at the right time. I ordered us another drink figuring that was thanks enough for any bartender.

Then I went on, "I've got a black horse, gentle as an old blind dog, but faster than that Old Fooler horse ever thought about."

"Is that a fact?" Nick said, wiping the sweat off his forehead and rubbing spilled whiskey on his hatbox belly.

"That's a fact."

Wrangler said, "I don't believe he's that fast myself."

"Now, Wrangler, I've told you and told you that I've run him against Old Fooler and it was a dead heat."

"That's good enough for me," said Nick.

"Sure wish somebody'd come along with some sporting blood," I said, and in a few minutes somebody with that very kind of blood rode up singing and yelling to beat hell. I'll be damned if it wasn't Vince Moore.

"Wonder what he's doin' in town?" I said.

"Looks drunk to me," said Nick.

"Naw, just headin' that way," said Wrangler.

It didn't take Vince long to tie that good-looking bay to a telephone pole, come in and have three drinks on me and Wrangler. In the time it takes to do that very thing a bunch of people had started to gather. Delfino Mondragon was in town with six months' back pay from sheep herding. Cowboys, farmers and all, gathered around knowing there was something going to happen. It did.

Delfino said, "Dusty, I feels like a leetle poker game."

He rubbed his black Mexican hair and said again, "A leetle games of chances."

Vince Moore whammed his glass down and said, "I'll

match that bay horse right there, for five-eighths of a mile, against any horse in the country!"

I said, "Why, Vince, I've got an old black horse that is just havin' a fit to run. In fact, if he don't get hisself in a race soon I figger he's just goin' to fret his poor self to death."

"I'm gonna give you the opportunity to save a horse's life. Cause I'll bet five hundred he cain't run as good as you think he can."

Well, all hell and things that were more fun broke loose. Everybody wanted to see this black.

I said, "Now just a minute, boys. When the time is right I'll have him ready. But first let's toast Hi Lo and all the fine people around it. To all the rich and all the poor, and let's go ahead and say that we hope some of them folks get to change places now and then, so they'll know how the other side feels."

I was so damn near out of breath it took me about a minute to tell Wrangler, "Get over to Rosie's and tip her off!"

Out he scooted.

Now old Vince had our five hundred and he was willing to bet it for us. Every dollar of it was to go on the bay.

As soon as I saw Wrangler and Rosie Peabody standing on the porch of the mercantile, I said, "Now, fellers, all of you line up down at the race track bleachers and I'll show you that black."

A big yell went up and everybody headed for the track. I took off for the brush. I saddled Old Fooler and told him, "Now, I've given you a reprieve from soap factories. I've kept you from being turned into dog food time after time. Now's your opportunity to pay me back. Just don't buck till I turn you loose at full speed."

Old Fooler looked at me and it was almost a kind expression that came on his face. I picked up the nearly empty jug Vince had left and settled its fate in one swaller. I had confidence.

As I rode out onto the track, the black hair gleamed where the varnish was on it. In the late fall like this, the other horses around had started putting on long winter hair. This black looked like he'd been combed and prepared for the Kentucky Derby. When we headed down the track I opened Old Fooler up, but at the same time I didn't let a millionth of an inch of slack come in the reins. If I had he'd have thrown me clear over the bleachers. That's exactly what I wanted him to do later.

As soon as I got around the track, where nobody could get close enough to examine Old Fooler, I looked over at the crowd. I could just hear them sucking in their breaths at this beautiful-moving, shiny race horse. They were all gathered around Rosie and Vince making bets. I knew the odds had jumped a mile as soon as they saw the horse. I circled once more holding him back.

Vince rode out and we lined up a little ways back from the bleachers. It was agreed that Rosie would say *go*. She gave me a big wink right out over them big teats Wrangler would enjoy so much, and I could feel my shins roasting by her fireplace already. I could just see Wrangler getting up around ten in the morning and saying,

"Dusty, some time this month we've got to get out and look for a stray cow." Why, after this race he would actually be able to buy and pay for the wedding ring. Wonderful, wonderful world!

"Go!"

We did.

I have been on some fancy-moving things in my life when you figure it all the way around, but it seemed like Old Fooler was going to outdo them all. He sure did. He passed the bay so fast I didn't have time to wave goodbye. When we hit the first turn, I pitched him the slack. I knew he would take rail and all when he left the track. Well, I damn near fell off because I was expecting to go one way but he kept running the other. *That* is right. Straight down the middle of the track we went.

Well at the end of the five lengths he was way, way ahead. But that was nothing, on his second time around he caught up with the bay from behind. Then, *that,* is right, *then* he jumped the fence.

He was beginning to slow down some when we hit Shorty Wilson's back yard. I'm sure glad it wasn't fenced. I could see a clothesline full of diapers coming right at us. I yanked on the reins as hard as I could and spurred even harder on one shoulder trying to turn him. It did. It turned him from a runner to a bucker. I ain't sure he meant to do it but he saved my life right there. That clothesline would have cut me right in half but Old Fooler, bless his heart, jumped so high that he hung the saddle horn over it and when he came down the line broke at both ends. I reached down trying to get hold of the horn, but it was too late. I prolonged fate about six or seven more jumps and away I went.

As soon as I could get the gravel brushed out of my eyes I looked up to see where Old Fooler was headed. That black-ass bastard was headed uphill for heaven, with two wings of wet diapers flapping the breeze.

It was almost dark before we finally caught Old Fooler and got him loaded in the pickup with the bay and the rest of us. I didn't ask Wrangler how Rosie felt, I knew. I didn't ask Vince how he felt, I knew. There was one of those silences that only the deaf can know.

We hit the highway and I thought it best to bypass town because Shorty Wilson's wife might want her diapers back and it would take me twenty-five years to gather them.

Finally Vince said, "You know what?"

"What?" old blabbermouth Wrangler asked.

"That Fooler horse is a go-gettin' son of a bitch!"

Six

I CAN TELL YOU one thing for sure, Jim Ed would just naturally see to it that we got in plenty of work. But old cunning me — I decided to help things along. The way I figured it, old Wrangler just had to get sure enough fed up with this ranch life, at least on the hired hand's end, before he'd get serious about marrying a rich woman.

A second hay cutting was about ready so I bobbed up and volunteered our best efforts. Now Jim Ed acted kind of surprised, but he acted a little bit tickled, too. It ain't the easiest thing in the world to get a couple of broke-up cowboys to put up hay twice in one year.

We took to riding a tractor; that is right. Hard to believe, but sure as hell true. Hooked to that tractor was a long hay-cutting blade that sliced her down slick. Then we came along and raked it up into wind rows and let it dry a couple of days in the hot sun. After that we drove a hay baler over it and the next thing you knew the fields were covered with pretty green bales.

Getting that hay into bales is just the first item; the second ain't quite so easy. It has to be loaded on a flat-bed truck, hauled to the stack lots, unloaded and stacked bale by bale in the form of a long pyramid. Lift. Lift. Lift. It takes some doing. Me and Wrangler were the doers.

After about two weeks of this I could tell my pardner was beginning to weaken. It was also getting boring doing the same thing over and over. That's just the way I wanted it. He even started talking *first* for once.

"This here work ain't fit for nothin' but mules," he said.

"You're right," I agreed.

"Well, how come we're doin' it then?"

I came right back at him since the whole thing was my bright idea, "Mules are too smart."

He grunted once and farted twice as he lifted a great big bale up to me on the stack.

We stacked right on into winter. And I might say there were times when I felt a little bit stupid for getting into this myself.

When we finished the hay-stacking, it was getting cold — plenty cold. In fact, we had washed and hung out a bunch of levis to dry and when Wrangler went to gather them in he had to turn them all upright to get through the bunkhouse door. He just leaned them up against the wall like sticks until they thawed out.

I slipped over to Jim Ed's that night and had a little talk.

"Jim Ed," I said, hoping his wife wouldn't come in the living room and examine my boots for foreign matter, as the town fellers say, "a lot of them posts around the stack lots are rotted so bad a feller cain't tighten the wires. If it comes a bad blizzard the cattle are just liable to walk right through that fence and tear down all them haystacks."

"You don't say?"

"Sure do."

"Well, Dusty, I'll put a couple of the odd-job boys on it right away."

"No need for that, Jim Ed, just sic me and old Wrangler on it."

He looked at me kinda sly-like and said, "Well, all right, but hadn't you rather ride fence, drive a truck and feed, or something a little more suitable for saddle-raised men?"

"No," I said, "by god you've saved me and Wrangler from goin' to jail and I'm goin' to see that we take on ever' dirty job you've got around here till we're even."

"Suits me," he said.

We had a couple of long iron bars and a couple of posthole diggers. I might as well say it now that I wanted to back out before the first day was over. The ground was already frozen down about eighteen inches as solid as Wrangler's skull. That meant that it took about an hour to bite out the first half of the hole and about two minutes for the rest. They had to be almost three feet deep to hold right. It was like digging in cement, and the unhandy part about posthole diggers, as I've mentioned before, is the fact that you have to pick them up every time you drive them at the ground. Otherwise they don't dig. Now if the soil hadn't been so rocky we could have used the automatic posthole digger on the back of Jim Ed's tractor. But if that had been the case I'd never have volunteered in the first place.

Our hands got a permanent bend in them. They looked just like hay hooks. It would take four or five gallons of Vince Moore's whiskey before I could pick up anything bigger around than an apple.

One day Wrangler tried to roll a cigarette. He finally gave up and just turned the sack up in his mouth and started chewing. He ain't so dumb sometimes at that.

Then it sure enough got cold. The ground was frozen plumb to the bottom of those holes.

"Progress we ain't makin', Wrangler. All we're doin' is wearin' out some good iron bars and posthole diggers."

He tried to answer but all I saw was a bunch of frost come out of his mouth. His little old razor-back eyes were watering so fast they looked like two fresh bullet holes in a bucket of water.

Jim Ed finally saw the waste and gave us another job. An indoor job at that.

"Now by god," I told Wrangler, "ain't we the two luckiest bastards this side of Hi Lo and the other side of hell?"

"It's all in the way you look at it," said Wrangler bitterlike.

That's what I wanted him to say. It's all that gave me the courage to carry on.

Now Jim Ed has got some mighty big barns. On different occasions, such as blizzards or heavy rains, during calving season, he keeps cattle in these same barns. He also feeds these cattle to keep them strong and healthy. There was soon no doubt in my mind but what they were healthy. That is as far as constipation was concerned. I'm flat-ass certain that Jim Ed never owned a cow that was bothered with this. In fact, after me and Wrangler had worked in the barns awhile I'd have bet my last saddle blanket that they all had the thin dirties.

Jim Ed had said the barn was big and airy. This was true. There was so much air and it got so full of manure dust that a feller had a hard time getting a fresh breath. We backed a truck into the barn and started out digging and shoveling.

Wrangler said, "This stuff is froze just like the rest of the world."

"Yeah," I said, "but it'll break off in layers." It did, by the millions.

One of us was swinging the pick while the other was swinging that scoop shovel full of frozen you-know-what on the back of a truck. When that truck had all it could handle one of us would drive down across the pastures and the other would scatter it out behind. Jim Ed said this fertilized the pastures. I figured the cows would have done a better job of it than we did.

Now Wrangler wasn't exactly complaining. It was more just stating facts. But it gave me hope.

"Dusty," he said, standing there with a scoop shovel full of fertilizer.

"Yeah?"

"Jim Ed lied."

"He did?"

"Yeah, he said it'd be warmer in here. Hell's fire the sun don't never shine in here."

"Well, I think you misunderstood him, Wrangler. He said we'd be indoors out of the wind and weather. And that's true."

He grunted.

Several months and millions of shovels later he stopped, holding the shovel in the same half-ready position and said, "Dusty."

"Yeah?"

"It's damn near spring and you know what we've been doin' for a livin' nearly all winter?"

I knew all right. I stopped and tried to see out of my blurry eyes, over my runny nose and fought to keep that hellacious taste from getting any further down my throat than it was. Just the same I said, "What?"

"Shit," he said, swinging the shovel kinda mad-like. "We're makin' a livin' shovelin' shit."

I could hear them wedding bells ringing clear as a police siren in spite of the half inch of you-know-what packed in each ear.

Hope had calved again.

Seven

YES SIR, things were looking up. The grass was sprouting green and tender, the birds were telling everybody about it, and Wrangler, like all the other animals on earth, had his mind on love. On top of that we'd soon be working the spring roundup and branding — having some real fun.

Then it happened. Jim Ed came snorting and blowing up in front of me and said, "That goddamn horse! That goddamn horse!"

"What goddamn horse?" I said, feeling the question unnecessary but doing my best to be polite.

"That Old Fooler. Who else?" he said, jabbing a finger about the size of a pool cue in my chest. "He's run off with five of my best thoroughbred quarter horses!"

"Five?"

"Five!"

"How'd he get out of the big horse pasture?"

"Opened the gate hisself," said Jim Ed.

"He wouldn't do that," I said, swallering my Adam's apple as fast as it jumped up.

"Naw," Wrangler said, not helping much.

"He sure did," Jim Ed said, "and he's gone into the wild horse country. You know damn well I aimed to show all those horses at the state fairs in Dallas and Albuquerque and the Grand National in Denver next January. That son of a bitch will cripple them horses till they won't be fit for coyote bait. That is if we ever get 'em back. Get 'em back," he said again and raised his great big buttermilk belly almost even with the third button on his vest. "You'll get 'em back or no pay, no town, no nothing."

Well just when things looked good, like I might get Wrangler in town while it was still spring and we had several months back pay to boot, and give us a chance to hunt up that rich woman, Old Fooler had sure enough fouled up our world. I might say this was not unusual, just disappointing.

Jim Ed went on, "Now, you're going to be held responsible for them five horses. By the time you work 'em out you'll be a hundred and ten years old."

This was not a good thing to hear. Me and Wrangler were trapped again. It was none of our doing, but there wasn't a lawyer in the whole damn state would take our case against Jim Ed Love. That's the way lawyers are. And even if we had won the case, the judge would have ruled in Jim Ed's favor no matter what. The power's where the money is and me and Wrangler were short as hell on that last item. Besides, everybody knows money's more important than people.

Another thing I knew bothered Jim Ed about those horses, it was his way of showing off, keeping his name on people's tongues and being a big shot all over the Southwest. He liked to read in the paper: Sammy Bar, registered quarter horse owned by Jim Ed Love of Hi Lo, New Mexico, Wichita Falls, Texas, and Stony Stump, Colorado, takes grand prize blue ribbon.

Now I can't say as how I blamed Jim Ed for that, but from my viewpoint I would like to see the name Wrangler Lewis shoved in that sentence at the right place.

As of now it was going to take some doing to get her done.

Now ordinarily Jim Ed would have made us camp out on the hard ground while we tried to gather those horses, but this time it was different. Jim Ed was going to lose face if he didn't show up at those scheduled horse shows. If I hadn't had love and marriage on my mind so strong, I would've spent the rest of my life hunting those horses just to mess up Jim Ed. As it was he let us have the pickup and all the saddle horses we could use.

Every morning we got up before daylight, caught our horses, loaded them in the pickup and drove about six miles into wild horse country. Then we mounted and rode our hind ends plumb raw (and that is hard to do with a cowboy's hind end) looking for signs of those strays.

There were only about twenty-five wild horses left up in the brush, and with Old Fooler and Jim Ed's five that made a little over thirty. Now figuring that they were scattered over something like fifty thousand acres, and figuring that there are one hundred and fifty trees to the acre — not counting all the bushes under them — it don't take no town feller to savvy that the odds were against us.

Every once in a while we would jump a little bunch. Away we'd go tearing through timber, ducking tree limbs (part of the time), dodging holes and crevices, and piling up over big rocks. We were working down lots of saddle horses and getting nowhere.

After about three weeks of this I told Wrangler, "Now, we've finally got Old Fooler's range located and we know where they're watering most of the time."

"Yeah," he said, humping up in the saddle and pushing his hat back.

"So, let's build a wild horse trap around the most used waterhole."

Old Wrangler said for an answer, pushing his hat back, "That sure is a skinny cloud up there."

I pushed *my* hat back and looked, "That ain't no cloud, that's a vapor trail."

"You mean there's a bird that leaves a trail in the sky?"

I just couldn't believe he was that dumb. On the other hand, he'd spent his whole life looking at the ground for cattle and horse sign. And this was the first time I could recall Wrangler looking at the sky. All he'd ever got from up there in the heavens was a leather-scorching sun, high winds and freezing blizzards. I gave him the benefit of the doubt and told him about jet airplanes.

"Oh," he said, and I couldn't tell whether he believed me or not.

Well, we built a wild horse trap that would have made

the best carpenter in the world proud of us. It was eight feet tall, the wire stretched tight as a whore's girdle, and the bottom two wires set back so we'd have a place to scramble to if the horses went on the prod. We covered this all over with heavy brush so you couldn't see the wire leaning on it. Then we swung the gate open and covered it just as good but with lighter material. We were pleased.

We hunted and we hunted. Twice we saw Old Fooler for a minute as he led the horses out of sight into the badlands. We were both peeled and bruised from top to bottom. And I might add our tempers were in the same shape.

Then the insult of all insults took place. It appeared to me to be as dirty as if somebody had slipped President Kennedy a mickey just before he spoke to the nation. Jim Ed called his Texas ranch for an airplane. They used them down there to scare cattle out of the brush. Not only that, but Jim Ed said we would have to pay for the pilot's time and gasoline. This was damn near too much.

Now our job, according to Jim Ed, was to stay up on a hill kind of concealed from sight as far as the horses were concerned and wait until this airplane drove them down into our trap, then we were to dash bravely down and close the gate. That sounded real fine, but so does a church bell at a funeral.

For three days we hunkered down holding our horse's reins, watching that tin bird fly around the hills.

"Now, ain't that something," I said, "a flying cowboy. I never thought the time would come I'd have to even get in the same county with one of them things. God-uh-mighty, the world's ruined, Wrangler. You ain't goin' to allow that on your ranch, are you?"

"Hell no," he said, "I'd chop the wings off that damn thing and make an outhouse out of it."

That was the way I liked to hear my pardner talk. Just then I damn near died. Here came that hombre and right under him was Old Fooler and a bunch of horses. The plane circled, sounding like a runaway rock crusher. But just when he was bending her in to shove them into the corral, Old Fooler turned and headed right up the side of a steep hill.

Now this is where the remains of the Wild and Woolly West brought sudden defeat to the modern age. That cow-pilot turned his plane and tried to climb in the air after Old Fooler. He topped out just behind him, but something got in his way. Two pine trees. The wings ripped off to each side and what was left of the plane rammed into a thick clump of oak brush and everything was out of sight — horses and all.

We rode over almost as fast as we could. I think if I'd hit my horse with the spurs just once we could have speeded things up. But me and Wrangler are both very tenderhearted cowboys and we never take advantage of dumb animals — just dumb people.

"By God he ain't dead," I said as I saw this pilot crawling out of the splintered plane.

"Oh hell," Wrangler said, then he corrected it when the pilot looked at us with spinning eyes. "Oh, hell is no place for airplane pilots."

"Where am I?" he asked.

"Well, now, I'll tell you, feller, you're a long ways from where you ought to be."

"Correct," Wrangler said.

"Shall we take him in or wait till Jim Ed comes after him, Wrangler?"

"Whatever suits you just tickles me plumb to death."

I knew he meant it, so I helped the pilot on behind the saddle and we started the first stages of delivering the lost to the fold. We found out that a cow-pilot's ass is not as tough as a cowboy's.

But I learned something that eased my pain a little bit. That plane was insured, so old Jim Ed couldn't make us pay for that, too. The way I looked at it we had saved the price of an airplane that day. That's lots of money even to bartenders and bank clerks. Oh, for the wild free life of a cowboy!

We kept right on hunting, and Jim Ed left us alone for a spell. Besides he and all the other hands were having a big time down at the spring roundup and branding.

Then it began to rain. Those black clouds built a roof over the mountains and sprung a leak. It rained enough to run an ocean over. It took us three hours to drive up to the hills with chains on the pickup and two to drive back home. That meant we had just a little over two hours a day to hunt wild horses. That's not much time in this big country.

The horses were slipping and sliding all over. A preacher uncle of mine told me he saw it rain so hard in California that a strong man could row a boat straight up in the air. I called him a liar. Now I wish he was here so's I could apologize.

"Wrangler, I didn't know a man could breathe water, did you?"

"There's lots of things a man can do we don't know about."

This wisdom was way over my head, so I shut my mouth before I drowned. I knew we were really in for it now. There would be water holes everywhere. Our chances of trapping that bunch of horses were about the same as a cowboy getting rich. Those are mighty long odds.

I decided since we were going to have to leave the JL without our pay, and since the cause of it was Old Fooler, that I'd shoot the low-lived son of a bitch. I started carrying a .30-30 on the saddle for that purpose.

Then the clouds busted up and the sun came dropping down on the land. The grass was stretching up and our backs drying out.

The fourth clear day, we rode up on a canyon so deep it must've been the roof to hell. And down in the bottom something was moving. After a long hard look we agreed that it appeared to be Old Fooler with a bunch of his slaves tagging behind. They were moving towards a shallower part of the canyon and towards our trap.

I said, "Let's ride like hell and get up ahead of 'em. They have to come out within a quarter mile of the trap. If we can't booger them into it I'll at least get a shot at that rottenhearted bastard of a roan horse."

Wrangler grunted.

We rode like hell. The wind was in our favor. We

waited and waited a whole bunch more. Then old Wrangler just pointed. His jaws were working silently like a single stem of grass in a high wind. I looked where he looked. My jaws worked, too. Old Fooler was slowly, as if it was his everyday job, leading that bunch into the trap. He walked right on in lazy-like. The others kinda hesitated, heads up, ears forward, snorting and trembling but they followed him in.

Well, old kindhearted us fairly shoved the steel in our horses' sides. I headed for the gate itself and Wrangler for the opening. We had a downhill run but even so four head broke out on us. But when the gate was shut tight we counted up and there besides Old Fooler and Jim Ed's five head were seven wild ones.

Old Fooler stood sleepy-like out in the middle with his eyes half closed. The rest just ran, and jumped and farted and turned like a bunch of airplane cowboys would've done. Plumb foolish-acting animals.

It took us quite a spell to rope each and every one of those seven wild ones and put a garter on them. (That is, we twisted a piece of rope so tight on one leg it cut off most of the circulation.) A three-legged horse is easier to drive. Then we turned them out and headed in. We left the pickup there. We could get it later.

It was damn near dark when I turned into the home gate with Old Fooler coming along nicely right behind and all the other horses scattered out between Fooler and Wrangler. Jim Ed was amazed. It was hard on him but he admitted the seven extra head would take care of everything.

We had a good night's sleep and he even sent another cowboy after the pickup. Then he paid us off the next morning.

We stuck the money in our pockets, loaded Old Fooler in the back of our own pickup and headed for a wedding. We didn't say goodbye to Jim Ed Love, but I sorta waved my fingers out in front of my face as we passed headquarters.

Eight

OLD WRANGLER really fought his head to get me to stop in Hi Lo.

He said, "I want a drink."

"That, I can understand."

"Well, stop."

"Cain't do'er, Wrangler."

"No brakes?" he asked, looking at the floorboard.

"No time," I said, "we got to get into Ragoon before night. We've done wore our welcome out in Hi Lo, and besides there ain't no rich women available since Rosie has deserted us."

Wrangler saw the truth of this, but he was still plenty thirsty.

Now nearly every time I'd been in town since I was eighteen years old I'd either been drunk, in a fight, in jail, or gone broke. Sometimes all four. It was all done in the interest of having fun, even though other folks seemed to think different. But for once I was going to try to handle these situations a little better — really use my thinker. I knew we had to get a pretty fancy hotel to meet rich women. That expense was okay, but this idea of gambling and giving all our money away the first day was out. Why, if we were careful, we could last a whole month and that ought to get the job done. Another thing that always set us back was those damn jails. It didn't matter how you got in, whether it was your fault or not the judge was going to say *guilty,* and fine you all the law allowed. That was considerable.

"You know, Wrangler, we had a hell of a time collectin' our wages," I said cautiously.

"Jim Ed's the *takin'* kind."

"That's what I meant. Now, when this is gone we may never get that big amount together again."

"It ain't likely."

"So, we got to be careful till you find that everloving woman with the big, fat purse."

He grunted.

I drove on, and then I saw the place. I knew it had to be the one. There it was, off the road a piece. And it said, COCKTAIL (I knew this was fancy talk for whiskey); PHONE (no need for them far as I could tell); TV (hell, Jim Ed had one of those but I'd never got to watch it); SWIMMING POOL (might come in handy for sobering up and taking a bath); DINING ROOM (kinda nice to have in an emergency). Yes sir, the RAGOON INN had it all. Not only that, it was plumb out on the edge of town so there was lots of scrub oak and cedar to tie Old Fooler until we could find somebody to pawn him off on.

I signed up for both of us at the register and paid a whole week in advance. The lady gave me a key and pointed out the room.

The Ragoon Inn was a big, old place made out of adobe bricks and there was so much glass in the main building two hundred people could have looked out all at once.

We drove the pickup out back and unloaded Old Fooler. Then we tied him to the pickup and gave him some oats. We'd have to feed and water the bastard every day until Wrangler got his marrying arrangements made — that is, unless we were lucky and he choked to death or something.

Then we went over to our room. It was the fanciest damn thing you ever saw. Two great big old beds, green rugs, just like a cow pasture after a good rain, a bathtub, a phone and one of them TV sets. There was a picture on the east wall of a naked lady standing there looking at a lake full of water. I walked over real close and took a better look but the woman was still too far off to tell much about her features.

Wrangler said, "Let's go get a drink."

"Not till we take a bath," I said, "and get on some clean clothes."

"I cain't wait," said Wrangler, and I could tell he meant it.

"Wait here just a minute," I said, "I'll go get us a bottle."

It was all right to get a little drunk the first night here but to be dirty and drunk both was not going to better our chances of starting a romance.

I went to the bar and brought back a bottle. Old

Wrangler was glad to see it. I guess this marrying idea had him a little upset. He took a big drink and said, "Ahhh." I could see that I was going to have to pioneer on this bath deal.

It didn't take me long. I'm a fast bath-taker. I ran a tub full of water for Wrangler. He took another slug of hooch, undressed and dived in.

"Wowwweeee, oh, oh, woowee."

I ran in to see what was the matter. I must have got the water a little hot. Old Wrangler was about to drown and it looked like when he got in he'd slipped and driven his big toe into the water faucet. I pulled his toe out and threw him out on the floor so he could get his breath. He was getting plenty of that, in fact the way he was choking and going on I believe he was getting too much air. His toe was all bloody and bent. I ran and handed him the bottle, feeling I had done my duty and more. Wrangler was going to be a problem.

I put on clean levis and a new shirt and told him, "I'm goin' on over to the bar. Come on over when you get ready."

I went up to the bartender and said, "A double," then I remembered my idea on making that money last and I said, "No, I'm too dry for that. Give me a beer."

He was a friendly feller with a belly as big as Jim Ed's but with a hell of a lot pleasanter look on his round, flat face. He smiled and said, "Whatever suits you is my pleasure."

I looked real hard at him a minute to see if he was kin to Wrangler. He talked some like him, but I knew he wouldn't admit it if he was.

I went over to the jukebox. Sure enough there was my favorite by Banjo Bill but I played some of those tunes by that Sinatra feller. I decided that was the kind of music old Wrangler ought to get married to. Then I got me a seat at a table halfway between the jukebox and the bar at a great big table. That beer was so good and that Sinatra feller so romantic-sounding that I plumb forgot about Wrangler, the time, and everything else. All of a sudden the jukebox went off and I threw my head up and there was a three-piece orchestra scattered out there on a little platform.

One of them started pounding hell out of a drum, another did the same to a piano and one of them was blowing into a horn with a lot of latches on it. It wasn't as good as that Sinatra feller but it wasn't bad either.

Then I realized the place was damn near full of people. I wanted to get up and go get Wrangler, but I was afraid I'd lose my table. I told the waitress just to bring me three beers so I wouldn't have to move for a spell. Time passed.

Then the waitress came up to my table followed by some women. Four of them to be exact.

"Could these ladies use your table? We're crowded. Miss Hopwell has a party of four."

I jumped up and started to run.

Miss Hopwell (I could tell she was the ringleader) said, "No, please, sit down. We'll just *join* you."

I plunked myself back down. Miss Hopwell pulled a coyote hide or something furry from around her neck and leaned forward. Her bosom slid out on top of the table like a couple of well-watered cantaloupes. If she'd been two inches shorter she couldn't have got within a foot of that table.

"I'm Miss Hopwell, Myrna Hopwell," she said. "And this," she said pointing a finger just plumb overloaded with rings, "is my niece Gloria, and these are her friends from college, Miss Devers and Miss Rollaway."

I nodded and said, "Howdy. I'm Dusty Jones."

"How is it you're called Dusty?" Miss Rollaway asked, rolling great big, green eyes like a hungry calf at a full bag of milk.

"I don't know," I said, "maybe it's because I'm such a fast bather."

They all laughed to beat hell. I had been dead serious, but it didn't take me long to find out two things about town women, they either sneer or laugh no matter what you say. This bunch was laughing. I tried to tell them about one of my uncle's dogs that thought he was a horse and ate grass till he starved to death. They laughed so damn hard I decided to shut up and dance. I asked Miss Rollaway first.

She was a mighty fine dancer, just snuggling up like a rubber hose and sliding round so easy I could hardly feel her touch the floor. Old Dusty was enjoying himself.

"Are you really a cowboy?" she asked, "I mean *really*. You dress like one, but so many people do, you know."

"Well, Miss Rollaway . . ."

"Jane," she said, and so did I.

"Jane, it's like this. If I said I was I'd be telling the truth, but if I said I was I'd be lying, too."

"I don't understand."

"Well, I used to be a fair hand and I reckon I could have been called some kind of a cowboy. You see, there just ain't no use for us anymore. They've got jeeps and airplanes, and tractors and pickup trucks," and I just went on and on.

"Oh," she said, "I think I understand."

I was glad she was a smart girl and had enough sense to shut up and dance. I danced with them all. Though I might say Myrna was somewhat of a problem. The way she was put together kind of made it impossible to scrunch up and get going. She was almost as tall as I was and I'm just about six feet.

I was doing my best when I heard a yell blast out across the dance floor that could come from only one person — Wrangler Lewis.

It wasn't hard to see that he'd finished the pint. He had his hat pushed way back on his head. The only time he did that was when he was sure enough drunk. He had wrapped his sore toe up in a pillowcase and there was sure as hell no boot on that foot. This made him walk a little short-legged but here he came just hollering and dancing a jig. I don't see how he could stand it on that sore foot, but it looked like he jumped higher on this one than the other. Me and Myrna quit dancing and so did everybody else. People on their way to the bathroom just clamped down and stopped to watch. Drinks were held an inch from the swaller hole without moving.

Wrangler ran right up to me and Myrna, circled about three times and then ran right under me and grabbed her.

"She looks just like Toy Smith, only better," he said. (Toy was a woman Wrangler had once had a big affair with.)

At first Myrna looked like she might booger and run, but when Old Wrangler threw his hat plumb across the bar and crowded up under that bosom and began to waltz her around slow and easy I knew we had something going. I slipped over to the bar and said to Dan (that was his name, Dan. I have always liked bartenders named Dan), "Dan," I said. "Dan, what's that woman do?"

He leaned over close and said, "Nothing."

That's all I wanted to know, because if she didn't do nothing she was either a whore or rich and I knew this one was rich. Wrangler would soon take care of the other part of that sentence.

Well, we all finally got settled back down at the table and Wrangler just moved in between Myrna and Gloria. He was talking low and fast. I didn't want to interrupt, but felt that now was the time to order a round of drinks on us. I could see that this crowd couldn't take many more. I was still being careful with our money.

Myrna said, "Martinis," to the waitress.

I'd never had one of them and I didn't figure Wrangler had, but I said, "All the way around."

When the waitress brought them old Wrangler acted as if he was going to pour it out. Then he said, "I ain't never had none of them before — none of them vege-tables or nothing." And he whipped her up and polished it off with one and a half swallers.

We had another. This time Myrna bought. Now I kind

of appreciated that. Not only because we were being thrifty but because I never figured why a woman shouldn't buy a drink if she had the most money.

I liked that Myrna, but Wrangler liked her a hell of a lot more. That was fine with me, he was the one we were trying to marry off.

Myrna took out a mirror and sort of powdered her round, pretty face, patted at that short curly brown hair and stood up. Old Wrangler let out another yell and grabbed the silky-looking coyote hide. Myrna kind of jumped back.

Wrangler said, "I wasn't goin' to steal it or nothin'. I was just goin' to help you put it on."

That just about broke Myrna and the other girls up. The romance was on. They said they'd call us the next day and make a date for cocktails.

"By god," I said, "that's fine," and shook hands all around. We walked out to the car with them. It was a fancy-looking son of a bitch. I'd never seen one just like it before. It had RR wrote on it. Just the same I had already figured this was the kind she'd drive.

Wrangler told Myrna to bend over and he gave her one of those hungry kisses and I could see her wiggling in her lace pants. I couldn't make up my mind which one of the girls to tell goodnight, so I just kissed them all.

Nine

IT HAD TAKEN about an hour of knob-twisting before we could see that TV. It sure was loud, but I was afraid to turn anything again because nearly every time I touched one of those buttons the scene would change to a West Texas dust storm, or a long line of barbwire fence without any barbs.

A little feller was jumping up and down swallering a soda pop yelling "Drink Pep, it has the pepper to make you peppy!" Then a man dressed up something like a cowboy — I could tell he was faking it by the way he laid his saddle down on the skirts, no real cowboy would ever do that — took a long drag on a cigar. He was stretched out by a campfire and he gazed off at the moon just like he'd put his brand on ten head of his neighbor's calves. Then a coyote howled and another look came on his face. This time like a man who had just slept with his first woman. That feller had lots of different looks. I never figured it out for sure but I think he was really a cigar salesman.

Then a program started where a bunch of women got up and bawled and shed tears and a real kindhearted feller gave them iceboxes, electric stoves and such like. He sure was a generous man. It sorta surprised me. I thought they killed all that kind off.

After a while, a woman called Lolane was interviewed by a man dragging a bullwhip around. He talked with the handle right up next to his mouth. When Lolane talked he held it up next to hers. I don't rightly believe you can say she talked. She just sort of grunted the words and it seemed like she spoke with her chest instead of her mouth. I couldn't place it but something about her reminded me of Myrna.

We watched some of those westerns. I'm still confused about that. It seems that these fellers are called cowboys, but they spend most of their time in town drinking whiskey — which just goes to show that they are a heck of a lot smarter than most real cowboys. When they are out in the country, they never do any of the work cowboys do, they just lay behind rocks and blow people's heads off. It's pretty silly, but kinda fun to watch. This TV is an amazing invention.

The phone rang. We both jumped up and I said, "Answer it, Wrangler, that's Myrna."

"I don't talk over them damn thangs."

So I picked it up and tried to be *proper* as the town fellers say, and said "Hello" instead of "Howdy."

"Wrangler?" came oozing out over the phone so sweet

I could feel the silver melting off my belt buckle.

"No. This here's Dusty."

"Oh, hi, Dusty. Could I speak to Wrangler?"

"No."

A silence came over the phone and she finally said, "Well, why?" sort of short-like. I knew I had to make things right quick.

"Well, it's like this, Myrna. Wrangler's got one of them things about telephones. You know, what do you call it where a man's afraid of something without knowin' why?"

"A complex," she said.

"Yeah, that's it," I said, "he's got a boogery complex about telephones."

"Oh, how delightful," said Myrna. "Just tell the little darling that I'll be over to the Inn in about an hour."

"Are the girls coming, too?"

"No, they've gone shopping. Jane said to tell you she'd see you tomorrow."

I was a little let-down at first; then I really perked up. This was going to speed hell out of things, her coming over by herself. It sure looked good. Our luck was on the go.

She got there about three-thirty that afternoon. We were the only ones there. We had some more of those vegetable drinks and I gave that singing feller I'd liked so much the day before a dime every time he opened his mouth. It seemed like he knew a big romance was busting out. He really did do a good job, Myrna had already reached over and laid her left hand — the one with all them blue-white rings on it — under Wrangler's beat-up old fist and she was rubbing it like it was made of gold. Wrangler just went on drinking left-handed. I was just getting ready to leave them alone when a feller in a fine-looking speckled suit and a hat that didn't have hardly any brim at all came buttin' in. He was sucking on a pipe and rubbing a little bitty mustache. I could tell he was the vice-president of something or other. It seems to me that those vice-presidents all walk and talk alike.

"Hello, Myrna, darling," he spouted out like a big bird. "Where have you been, my dear? I've looked all over for you, precious. You look just divine, my pet. Simmmm-ppply divine!"

By god, I never heard anything like it. Less than thirty words and he had already called her darling, my dear, precious and divine. That man was a flattering fool. If he stayed an hour I wondered if he'd repeat himself.

I was surprised at how impolite the bastard was, considering his raising and all. He sat down at our table without even being introduced, much less asked. He just kept asking questions and answering them himself.

"I bet you've been to another of your flower shows. Of course you have, sweet. No, no. Let us see. Were you playing bridge at Esther's? That's it. I knew it, dumpling."

Myrna tried to say something but there just wasn't much use. I saw her pull her hand away from Wrangler's. I could tell she didn't want to.

On and on he rattled. New York and Hollywood, London and San Francisco kept coming up over and over.

Finally he kind of half covered his face with his hand and said, "Why, Myrna, you little rascal, leave it to you.

Wherever did you find these quaint gentlemen, my love?"

Myrna tried again. "Well, I . . ."

"Why on earth haven't you introduced us?" But before she could answer, the son of a bitch ordered *himself* a drink.

Well, I'll tell you this, I hated to spend the money, but I ordered three more vegetable drinks. This man, we finally found out that his name was Limestone Retch, kept right on blabbing.

"I wish the Monroes would improve their tennis court. They've talked about it for years. Louise is probably too busy in town, you know what I mean?" he said, looking sideways and flaring his nostrils like he'd just been told he was more of a dude than the Duke of Windsor. I could tell by that little "you know what I mean" business that somebody's throat was bleeding.

We had some more drinks. The sun was about to set. Some other people had come into the bar by now. The blabbing went on. He was getting a little drunk now and started telling dirty jokes. I heard every damn one of them when I was a kid. He was the only one who thought they were funny. He laughed so hard every time he finished telling one I kept hoping he'd bust something.

All of a sudden Wrangler said, "Do you swim, Limestone?"

"Wha . . . er . . . sure, but of course, all over the world, the finest places, Capri, Morocco, the Isle of . . ."

"Well, it's a damn good thing," old Wrangler said kind of humping up, "because I'm just fixin' to stir my drink with you."

Limestone swallered.

I swallered.

Myrna grinned sick-like.

I could see our ranch going to hell one way or the other right here. It was obvious that Limestone had just enough sense to understand that Wrangler was making headway with Myrna and it was just as obvious that Limestone had the same plan.

Wrangler was getting up on his sore foot, and I could tell he was going to do some damage to this vice-president's mustache.

I jumped up and ran around and said, "Come on, Limestone, I want to show you my horse. You ride, don't you, Limestone? Well, that's good. You'll like the looks of this ole pony. He's a dandy. Just wait till you see him." By god, it was my time to talk and I was doing it.

In the shank of the day I could still see Old Fooler's steel-muscled hind end sticking around the edge of the pickup. I let Limestone stumble out ahead of me and the damned fool walked around behind Old Fooler without speaking to him. Seems to me that as brilliant as this bastard's conversation was he'd have learned something in school. Damn near everybody knows you have to speak to a horse when you walk up behind him, otherwise he kicks. This is a throwback to the millions of years of time they spent being slipped up on by lions, tigers and such.

Blooey.

Whop.

Ooommmp.

Thud.

There wasn't much talking going on now. Limestone was stretched out there holding his belly and looking for some air. Old Fooler was jumping around, snorting and kicking right out over Limestone's head. But Limestone didn't know it. All he knew right then was that two cannon balls in the shape of horse's feet had whammed him in the belly.

I poured a half bucket of water on him that was too dirty for Old Fooler to drink and he kind of woke up. I just couldn't get that feller to talk to me. I tried and I tried. So, I thought to keep him from getting lonesome I ought to voice an opinion or two.

"Now, Limestone, you might think that hurt, but that's just like a loving mother rubbing powder on a week-old baby compared to what old Wrangler'll do to you. Leave Myrna alone. Do you hear me?"

He nodded and I could tell that the dumb bastard understood, so I helped him to his feet and he left, stumbling off without his pipe. He still wasn't saying anything. The quietened type I reckon.

I heard him drive off in one of those little peanut-looking cars. Then in a minute I could see Wrangler and Myrna heading for our room. I got my bedroll out of the pickup and told Old Fooler, "You have now been granted another week of life, you matchmakin' son of a bitch!"

Ten

THE SUN was up when I crawled out of my bedroll. I fed, and even brushed, Old Fooler down. This made him suspicious. He watched me close.

I said, "No, sir, Old Fooler, today we are friends. This here day will be celebrated sometime in the great future just like the Fourth of July, as the day the cowboys won. Whiskey'll run like spring rains, bands'll play and bribed judges and crooked lawyers will all make patriotic speeches."

I could tell Old Fooler didn't much believe me. Besides I decided I'd better shut up before I got to sounding like Limestone Retch.

I heard a noise so I looked around the edge of the pickup and saw Myrna leaving. She stepped off down to that big RR car like a madam with a full house. By god, I was nearly as happy as she was.

I dogtrotted over to the room. I just couldn't wait any longer.

By god, old Wrangler was learning fast. He was sing-ing in the tub and soap was spilling out all over.

"Come in, Dusty, you no-good son of a bitch." That was the best thing Wrangler could say to a friend. I was happy.

I started to ask him how it went, then I saw the horrible condition of the bed and knew the deal was cinched.

"Did she get excited when you proposed to her, Wran-gler?"

"She sure did. The poor thang fell out of bed!"

Things picked up from then on. Wrangler and Myrna went around everywhere together. She bought him a bunch of new tailor-made suits, shirts and boots. He even went so far as to wear a new hat when he was with her. They took in the opera, art shows, cocktail parties and such.

I made myself scarce during this period. Knowing they had plenty to do alone. In the meantime I had me three college girls to escort. The trouble was, for some reason, I liked this Miss Rollaway better than the others. The reason was hard to come by, because they were all pretty and paid their way.

I was learning fast just like Wrangler. I got to where I could operate one of those phones like a regular mechanic. I'd call her up and have her meet me somewhere without her friends. This helped to keep my spirits up while I waited for the great wedding to take place.

Finally Myrna had us all out to her house. It was out on the opposite side of town from the Ragoon Inn. She called it "the suburbs." Now the first thing I can say is that the house covered a whole lot of country. The rooms were all on different levels so it was hard to get from one to the other without falling down. This was impossible after a few of them vegetable drinks. It was one of those old Mexican adobe houses all smarted up with newfangled stuff — pictures, statues, pianos, bathrooms and bars. There were enough Navaho rugs on the floor to stock a curio store.

The outside was something to tell about, too. In the back yard was a big swimming pool all hemmed in with sandstone rocks. The same kind of sandstone I'd spent my whole life riding over and falling on, and here they'd found it useful. Paths wound around everywhere. Little fields of flowers were scattered all over. Myrna really loved those flowers. We were introduced to every plant on the place

"Look at my little darlings," she said, and reached out almost touching them. She talked to them like they were her kids.

All I could think of to say was, "Sure pretty."

Old Wrangler improved some on this. He said, "Mighty pretty."

I had heard she was an expert flower woman. I don't know if this meant she was an expert grower, smeller or raiser. It wouldn't have surprised me if she was good at all three.

We were sitting out by the swimming pool after our tour in the warm sun.

"Wrangler," I said, "when I was a kid all the poor folks lived on the edge of town; now it's the rich part."

"Everything changes," he said, firing up a cigar as long as a ruler and putting his brand-new kangaroo boots up on the table.

"Yeah, it sure does," I said, feeling happy at Wrangler's quick adjustment, but at the same time a little uneasy, too.

Myrna had the maid bring us a pitcher of drinks. I didn't know what they were and I damn sure wasn't going to ask. A man that would question free drinks ought to be hung in an outhouse like Wrangler said.

Myrna said, "Dusty, dear, would you like to bring your horse out here? We have the stables, you know? They're terribly empty. I just haven't had time to ride the last few years with the flowers and all to look after." She gazed out at all those short, tall, bunchy, skinny, red, yellow, white and purple flowers with the same look she had in her eyes for Wrangler. I knew the only competition he'd ever have would be those flowers.

"I sure would appreciate that, Myrna," I said. "It's some trouble over there at the Inn."

"You won't even have to worry about caring for him," she said. "I'll have the handy man do it."

Now by god ain't that a dinger. In a way I was already a foreman. Life sure enough looked good.

My main worry had been about Wrangler's conduct but like most of the things in the world I had strained my poor brains for nothing. In fact, if there was any worrying to do it was about him overdoing it.

One morning I saw him pick up a can of stuff and mash a button. Something sprewed out. He shot it under both arms, then sprayed some of it on his hair and combed it back slick and shiny. I slipped over directly and stole a look at the label. It was the same stuff they'd been advertising on TV: MASHO, FOR SMELLY MEN. PROTECTS ALL DAY. That's what it said on the can.

This might be all right for old society-climbing Wrangler but I'll be damned if I was ever going to admit I smelled that bad. But just the same he was doing better than all right. She was running by to pick him up in the RR car every little bit. And when she wasn't there the cockeyed phone was ringing. But the best sign of all was when she started handing him out a bunch of those brand-new fifty dollar bills. Then I knew old Wrangler had her as helpless as a tail-swinging monkey in a forest of sharp-spined cactus. That's to put it plain.

One day Wrangler came running in with a newspaper, yelling, "Look here! Look here! I got my name in the newspaper."

It said: "An engagement party will be held announcing the coming wedding of Miss Myrna Hopwell, Dime Store heiress (her third) to Mr. Wrangler Lewis (his first) of Hi Lo, New Mexico. Miss Hopwell lives on her estate near Ragoon, New Mexico, and is a specialist in mountain grown flowers. Mr. Lewis is engaged in the cattle and horse business."

"I never thought I'd see the time I'd get my name in the newspaper."

"Me neither," I said, but I was just about to bust a gut with pride. This here made it official. Nothing but a plague could keep me from being Wrangler's foreman now. I could just see the fat cattle and fine horses all over our ranch, and me riding around on the best horse in the country telling other people what to do. Oh, I'd be a decent son of a bitch about it. No dirty stuff like Jim Ed Love, but it would be a whole lot better boot to wear. I'll swear it looked like the improvements in this world would never end.

Eleven

THE ENGAGEMENT party brought on a pack of new experiences for me. I've never seen such a thing in my life.

At one end of the living room, on a flower-covered platform built for the occasion, was a four-piece band Myrna had — as she put it — "engaged." The other side of the room was nearly filled up with a twenty-foot long table running over with turkeys, hams and plate after plate of grub I never saw or heard of before. And besides a bowl of punch as big as a horse trough, she had two bartenders behind the bar working themselves plumb rattle-headed trying to empty all those whiskey bottles. They did a good job, but it took them all night.

Yes sir, this was sure as hell going to be a party of engagements all right.

People were as crowded as fingers on a closed fist and more kept coming in. Myrna had Wrangler by the arm introducing him to all the people around the room.

All these new faces made me nervous. I was really wishing Miss Rollaway and her friends could have made it home from school for this blowout. I finally eased my way over and told the bartender to fill my glass.

"Soda water?" he asked.

"No, whiskey," I said. I turned that old glass up and drank'r so empty it looked like a brand-new one.

"Again?"

"Again!"

It wasn't a very big glass but I felt more sociable and I had learned why they sometimes called these get-togethers cocktail parties.

A feller walked up to me and said, "How do you do, old chap? I hear from Myrna you are in actuality a real, working cowboy."

I didn't want to get into any more discussions trying to tell this Englishman I was an ex-cowboy, so I just said, "That is right."

"Well, it is my pleasure to introduce myself. I am Sir Shambles, Ambassador at Large for Her Majesty. I'm now stationed in the Islands. I flew over for Myrna's party. Good girl. Old friends, you know?"

I didn't know, but I nodded my head and took a sip of whiskey.

"When I heard she was marrying one of the cow people I could hardly contain my interest. You see we English pioneered the cattle industry in America."

This here did sort of set me back on my hunkers. I'd never really thought about how it started. It seemed like to me it had always been here, long as I could remember, at least.

"Is that right?" I said.

"Indeed, it is, my dear fellow. The old XIT Ranch in the Texas Panhandle is only one of the rather large estates instigated by English capital."

I took a liking to this feller right then and there, but before I could get some real friendly talk going a herd of fat old women ran off with him, just introducing one another so fast I thought they were going to tear the poor feller in half.

I learned something else I didn't know — just get you a drink and stand in one place. All kinds of folks will come up and talk to you. If you move about it becomes *your* responsibility to start the talk.

This feller walked up to me and said, "I'm Jack Garfield."

"I'm Dusty Jones."

"I'm vice-president of . . ."

I knew it, by god, I knew it. Another one of them. I started to bust him right off and then I remembered I was on good behavior till after the wedding.

"I was just over at Judge Malhead's yesterday. Know him? Fine man. Great person. We're just like this. He said to me, 'Jack,' he said, 'we've been friends a long time haven't we?' 'Yes, we have, Judge.' 'Well,' he said, 'I'm going to let you in on a big thing. Something *really* big. Get me? You have to swear by the utmost secrecy not to let this out.' I looked the judge straight in the eye and said, 'Judge, you know me better than that.' 'All right, Jack,' he said, 'here it is. They're going to build a new electronic plant here in Ragoon. It's going to be put on the Smith property.' Well, I'll have you know, Mr. Jones, that *I* just

this morning closed a deal for all the surrounding property for *our* company. How do you like that? Fast work,
eh?"

"Well, I'll be a goddamned chicken-stealing, lamb-killing coyote," I said.

This seemed to please him because he said, "Mr. Jones,
if you ever need anything, any little favors, just let me
know. I can get to the judge anytime. Of course there are
certain little favors one has to give in return. Convention,
you know. Just business. Plain business."

For a minute there he had me thinking he really meant
it. But when he got to that "certain favors" part I knew
I was out.

He was starting out on another one of his smart deals
when this fat woman came up and started talking to
him.

I slipped over sideways but before I could take another
drink one of those fat women grabbed me. Her eyes
bugged out like two tiny burned-out light bulbs. She was
wearing so many necklaces they pulled her forward. I
had the notion to give her a push and get her straightened
up.

"My darling" (by god the world was full of darlings).
"I'm so glad for Myrna. She's really been lonely these last
years. Of course, she has her flowers and uh, of course, all
those millions to comfort her. And uh, you will be good
to her won't you, darling?"

"Yeah," I said.

"She needs someone she can trust, you know? And uh,
someone to lean on in time of tribulation. Of course, we

all do," she said and kind of shook like something was binding her.

"I ain't the one," I said.

"Whatever do you mean?" she said, and gave me a look that would have scared a natural born coward flat to death.

"I mean, I ain't marrying Myrna."

"Well!" she said and hustled off twisting all over trying to get out of that bind.

I decided it was time I changed locations. I went to the bar. Then I squatted down behind a little tree planted in a great big bowl. Three or four people were talking at once. Finally one of them got louder than the others.

"I tell you the evils of the world are rooted in organizations: communism, religion, marriage and yes, even capitalism."

"Capitalism an organization?" somebody said.

"Exactly. You know we all know. We're afraid to admit it. Look at all the organized good we've done to all the primitives in the world. They were happy until the capitalist and the communist started showing them the difference. Death, pain, love and beauty were all accepted for what they are — simply part of the universe. But now we've ruined them. We've educated them. Ha!" He was getting louder all the time. "The only truth, the only government worthwhile has been found in a monarchy."

Since I didn't savvy a thing they were talking about I got up and made another move. Across the room, poor old Wrangler was still going strong on that handshaking.

Marrying a rich woman wasn't quite as simple as I thought.

I saw a lonesome-looking feller sitting on a window seat. I ambled over and said, "Howdy."

He looked up at me out of sneaky, sad eyes, rubbed his beard and nodded.

"Nice party, ain't it?" I said.

"It will do, I suppose."

"You live around here?" I asked, trying to get something going.

"Oh, temporarily. New York is my home. I'm just here on, well, shall we say research."

He waited like he wanted me to ask him what kind of research. But I didn't.

So he said, "I'm a poet."

Well I'll be damned if he didn't look and act just like I thought a poet would. Course I don't know any poets.

There was a commotion outside around the swimming pool. People had started pushing one another into the water with all their clothes on. They had to get pretty drunk to do it, but it was happening just the same. They were laughing real loud like this was the funniest thing in the world. I was getting a little worried about my sense of humor. Maybe I was losing it.

I turned back to the poet and said, "Come on, let's grab us a girl and dance and holler and have some fun."

He looked at me another minute and said like it was making him sick, "You call *that* fun?"

Well before I could grab me a girl, a great big husky man with a bowtie on walked up and said, "There's no use. They are just no good."

"Huh?" I said.

"Thass right. They are *no damn good.* She's gone to her aunt's. Sheesh taken the kids. My kids," he said, and started crying and rubbing his round face.

"Who?" I asked.

"My wife. She won't be my wife any longer. I just can't understand it. When we first got married we were so happy. I didn't get to stay home much. The business was just starting. Had to make a go of that. A man's got to make a go of that, hasn't he?"

"I reckon he has," I said.

"Well, he does. You just can't get along unless you make a go. You're left out. I worked sixteen hours a day making it go. It went," he said, sniffing and looking up at the ceiling. "Yeah, it went. I just don't understand it. I gave her everything. Clothes, cars, one of the best homes in town. She had a maid. We made all the clubs in town. Look," he said, and pulled out a billfold that unfolded like an accordion. "Look. You see these?"

"Unhuh. What are they?"

"What are they? Credit cards, that's what they are. Look. I have five different gasoline cards. Three diners, two . . . one . . ." and he just kept rattling "This is my country club card and I belong to the Masons, Kiwanis and Lions. Now, if that isn't proof, where is it?"

When he said "proof" I thought maybe he was in some kind of trouble with the law. But that wasn't it at all. It was his wife he was trying to prove something or other about.

All that whiskey I'd drunk made me feel helpful, so I said, "You have to make love to 'em ever' day."

"Every day?"

"Ever' day."

"I don't have time for that."

It was my turn to talk so I said, "And that ain't all you've got to do. You've either got to beat hell out of them or make 'em ragin' mad about something at least once a week."

"You do? Why?"

"I don't know why and I don't care why, but that's the only way they love you."

"Oh! Oh, I couldn't do that," he said, "she'd sue me. Why she'd take everything *I* own!"

I wasn't doing this feller much good so I just walked off looking for someone else to help. It didn't take long. This little woman, or girl I reckon you'd call her, just latched onto me and turned the most pitiful set of eyes up to me I nearly ever saw. She looked kinda like a kitten that had just been spanked by a mouse.

"He's done it again," she said.

"Lord a mercy, what?"

"Got himself tied up for another five years. Says he'll be president of the company in another five years."

"What is he now?"

"He's vice-president now. First vice-president."

"There you go," I said.

"There you go where?"

"Oh, nothing."

"Well, I told him that I'd like to hear something just once besides business and promotions. Just once. And another thing I didn't tell him about is all those silly dinners he makes me go to. I'm supposed to smile at some numbhead all evening and listen about his conquests of the business world. Of his clever little subtilities to get and keep the advantage over his cohorts."

"His what?"

"His associates."

"Let's go get us a drink," I said.

She patted her smooth hair and said, kind of surprised, "Well, all right."

I no longer had to tell the bartender how I wanted my drinks. And I said, "The lady will take one just like it."

She said, "How do you know I'll like it?"

I said, "I don't, but if you're goin' to drink with me that's what you'll drink."

She smiled, "I'm game."

We had another drink. I don't hardly think she was used to this kind of cocktail hour, so I just eased her around and danced with her.

She said, "My, that was nice."

"It sure was."

Then she started blabbing again. "It's to the point now that we're sleeping in separate bedrooms."

I said, "I just can't believe it. Why I never heard of such a silly thing."

"It is true," she said, and tears started running down on her pretty little cheeks.

Here was somebody I could help. I led her around through all those drinking, talking, arm-waving people and down aways to a dark room. I couldn't find a bed in it but it didn't hold things up much. I just grabbed her and kissed her and threw her down on the rug. All she ever got to say was "No . . . noooo."

It wasn't long till this woman was feeling a whole lot better. I even felt some better myself.

She told me, "Thanks."

And I said, "Glad to do it."

I let her go back to the crowd first, then in a bit I followed.

Everybody was looking over towards a sure-enough fancy woman. I'll be a chicken-stealing, lamb-killing coyote if it wasn't that Lolane I'd seen on TV the other day.

Myrna was introducing old Wrangler to her. In a minute he threw his head up and looked around until he spotted me. He waved one of his short, heavy arms for me to come over. I went.

That Lolane's hair was so blond her shadow looked bleached, but everything else seemed real. Real good, in fact. Everything except the feller that was with her. He was about a foot taller than me. His hair was slick and black and so shiny in places it looked like he had deep barbwire cuts in his head. He just smiled and smiled and smiled.

"Hello there," he said to everybody he met, and he flashed that row of white teeth till I thought he was going to split a lip.

Well, sir, the next thing I knew I was dancing with Lolane. It was a real pleasurable thing to do. She was a little silly at first saying such things as . . . "My, it's hot in here, isn't it? I just think Myrna's house is too too. I'm starting a new picture next week. It has the most divine cast, and the script is just too too. I'm tired of it though. Some day I'm going to settle down in a little place like Ragoon and just do nothing but read."

This last kind of made me taste the steel bits in my mouth. There were so many things a woman like this could do to have fun besides read. Damn near anybody could read. Even old Wrangler knew almost half the words in the Ragoon newspaper.

Poor girl. Everybody stared at her except her husband; he was over talking to the poet. They were flinging fingers at one another in what looked to me like an insulting manner. Course you couldn't tell about that cause one of them smiled all the time and the other one never did.

When the music stopped, everybody gathered around us. They kept wanting to meet her or say something to her or in some way be recognized.

"By god," I said right in the middle of the next dance, "come out here. I want to show you my horse." I'd heard about these artists and fancy folks showing their etchings. Well, I show my horse.

"Reckon your husband'll miss us?"

"Oh, he's not my husband. Why I haven't been married in weeks. Ray's gay. It just looks good for us to be seen together."

"Yeah," I said, "he does seem kind of gay. Smiles all the time."

"You're kidding," she said.

I couldn't figure how she figured I was kidding so I just dropped that subject.

She held tight to my arm and snuggled up a little as we walked down the path to the stables. Now I'm not one to carry on much about scenery, but man, what a night.

Old Fooler was standing near the middle of the corral in the bright moonlight with his head down and he didn't bother to look up.

"There he is," I said.

"Is he a good one?" she asked. "Is he spirited?"

"Yes, Miss Lolane, you are looking at one of the most spirited animals on earth."

"Oh, that's just too too," she said, and kind of shook all over. "I made a western," she said. "Did you see it?"

"No, I don't reckon so. What was it called?"

"*We Fit,*" she said. "It flopped."

A coyote howled off in the hills behind the stable. "My goodness," she said and crowded up closer. "He sounds like he's crying so so sad."

"No, ma'am, that animal's laughing."

"Laughing?"

"*That* is right."

"Well, what on earth does the poor thing have to laugh at?"

"Why, he's laughin' at us people."

"Why would he do that?"

"He's smarter, that's why."

"You're kidding," she said.

Now I was beginning to like Lolane, but I could see right now I was going to have to get her over the idea I was always kidding. So, I took her in the corral to get a closer look at my spirited horse. Then I showed her my saddle where the moonlight shot through the stable door. Then I threw the saddle blanket down in that pale blue shaft of moonlight.

She said, "What did you do that for?"

Bless that old coyote's laughing heart, he howled again before I could answer. She made another one of those shaky snuggles and I gathered her up right against my levi buttons.

She made out like she was going to pull away, but I could feel her hoping I wouldn't let her. I didn't. I took hold of that little pouty red mouth with mine. She wanted this. I felt up and down her back until my hand found that dress zipper, then smooth as silk I slid it down.

Stars above! When I stepped back, that low-hung dress just dropped off on the ground. That dress had been her entire wardrobe. We dropped right down beside it onto the saddle blanket. Now I knew why she reminded me of Myrna. They were so big it took both hands to give one of them a good feel. But no problems, I have two hands.

"Ohhhh," she said, and by doggies we made love.

At first she acted a little like she was in the habit of doing it just to be nice, but in a minute more she was loving because she liked it.

It was a beautiful, soft, warm place so we lay awhile longer and let the goodness soak all through us.

After a little, she put her mouth to my ear and whispered, "That horse is watching us."

I looked around and sure enough there Old Fooler stood with his ears pitched forward. I whispered back, "It's all right, he won't tell anybody."

All of a sudden, I jumped up, grabbed her by the hands and pulled her to her feet. Then I just turned her around in that beam of moonlight and looked. She was a hell of a lot prettier than her pictures.

I walked around and took a look at her rear. It was about the prettiest thing I'd ever seen. Old Wrangler is a milk-cow man. He likes big-chested women. Well they're just fine, but I'm more of a quarter-horse man myself. It's those hindquarters that set me to going.

Then I circled her while she trembled and shivered all over. She was breathing so hard I got worried and thought I better get her bedded down again.

It was better than before. By god if this woman had been out of the spotlight awhile and had the right training she'd have been the champion lover of the whole United States.

We rested again.

Then she said, "Darling, hand me my dress." When I did, she kind of straightened it out and started trying to put it on while still sitting down. She did it!

I said, "I'll be a goddamned chicken-stealing, lamb-killing coyote!"

She said, "Nothing to it. Experience in the dressing room."

Just like I figured, all she needed was experience.

We got up and told Old Fooler goodnight. I could have sworn he had an evil grin on his face. She walked along holding my arm, her head kind of over on my shoulder. She said, "That was nice. It was real."

I didn't say anything.

The next thing we heard was old Wrangler taking on

out in the patio. I kind of hurried up, getting a little
scared. Here we were just a half mile from heaven and I
didn't want anything to happen.

A crowd was gathered around the pool. Almost everybody had already either jumped in or been thrown in.
I reckon this foolishness is what gave Wrangler the idea.
He was standing at the edge of the pool with Myrna hanging on to his arm. She looked a little drunk, so I don't
think she was being loving or comforting at the moment,
but mainly trying to stand up.

The Englishman was standing close by with a big wad
of money in each hand taking bets. "Now," he said,
"since my countrymen were the pioneers, yea, the very
creators of these cow people, and since Mr. Wrangler
Lewis is one of that fast-vanishing breed, I will say with
all sincerity and implicit faith, I believe he can do what
he says! Step right up and place your bets!"

Everybody was looking for gambling money. The
vice-president was trying to make a bet on the strength of
his credit cards.

All of a sudden Wrangler downed a big vegetable
drink, threw the glass up in the air and started singing:

> *Jesus loves me this I know*
> *For the Bible tells me so.*
> *He will wash me white as snow*
> *Dirty, dirty job for Jesus.*

Yes sir, this society bunch had given Wrangler religion.

I grabbed the Englishman's shoulder and asked,
"What's he goin' to do? What're you all bettin' on?"

He looked at me and said, "My dear fellow, your

pardner maintains he is going to walk across the pool."

"My god, he thinks he's Jesus!" I yelled, and tried to get through the crowd to stop him. I was too late. He had bent down and picked up one of those loose sandstone rocks right out of the patio floor. Then he walked to the edge of the pool and stepped off. What with holding that big rock and the fact he couldn't swim, he went right to the bottom. And in the deepest part too!

The crowd was quiet.

Myrna screamed, "Save my love!"

I grabbed her and said, "Look!" For there in that pale green water stepped old Wrangler. He walked clean across the bottom of that pool, and when he got to the shallow end his head came out like a turtle's. He was blowing to beat hell. But who wouldn't be, he'd been walking uphill.

The deed was so full of courage that nobody argued any technical points. Instead they hauled him out of the water and a great shout rose from their drunken throats.

Myrna cried, "My hero!"

The Englishman gave Wrangler half the winnings and I just walked over and patted Lolane on her beautiful butt.

It couldn't have been a finer world.

Twelve

On this particular morning, we got up by inches.

I said, "All the time I thought I'd been pourin' them drinks in my stomach, they'd been goin' in my head."

"I feel like I've been pulled through a half-inch water pipe a mile long," Wrangler answered, sitting up trying to get the hair out of his eyes. "Anything to drink around here?"

"Nothing but about an inch and a half of stale wine in that bottle over there," I said, pointing to a dresser.

He got up, weaved over and stared at the bottle. "I'd rather drink carbolic acid than that stuff," he said, and picked up the bottle and drained her dry with one swaller. I thought he had a funny-looking face till now. But the one he made after that wine was just too damn bad for even his best friend to look at.

I got up, put on my pants and boots and stumbled down to the coke machine. I felt bad. I had enough of this drinking to do me for nine years. Maybe forever.

I put a dime in the machine and got my coke. When I got back to our door I said, "Wrangler, want a coke?"

"Hell no, what time is it?"

I looked at the sun, "Oh, about eight-thirty."

"The bar opens in thirty minutes," he said.

"You ain't goin' to drink again today, are ya'?" I said. "Hell, the wedding's tomorrow."

"Well," he said, making good sense, "we've been cele-bratin' the engagement for nine days now, we ought to toast the weddin' itself for at least one."

I couldn't argue. The best thing I could do was see that he didn't get too drunk. Now that was going to be a grind.

We started out by having a couple of beers in the Inn. Then we ordered three eggs and a big chunk of ham with some black coffee. The world began to look a little bit like it had the day before.

I knew Myrna was busy getting ready for the wedding, and if she wanted Wrangler she'd look for him at the Inn. I didn't want to take a chance on anything happening so I said, "Come on, let's hunt another bar. This'n here is tired of us."

"Whatever suits you just tickles me plumb to death," he said, being agreeable as long as I was looking for a bar.

Well, by ten o'clock that morning we had found one a lot closer in town. It was dirty and dark and run by a Mexican. I figured old Wrangler would kinda like this. It's the only kind of joint he's used to. But he wouldn't say much when I talked. Maybe this high living was spoiling him.

"Well, tomorrow it'll all be over," I said, feeling better by the minute. "You'll have a good-looking rich woman. One you can truly love. That's cake with icing, boy. In a few days we'll buy that nice cow outfit and I can go to work running it for you. I bet you never thought that would happen to us, did you, pardner?"

At the word "pardner" he threw his head up, grunted and motioned to the bartender to bring us another round.

"Tell you what we better do, Wrangler. Soon as we get our ranch tied up, we better start building us a rodeo arena. On Sunday afternoons we can invite the local boys over for calf roping and maybe a little wild-cow milking and bronc riding."

"Had all the bronc riding I want." He was staring at a Mexican gal that must have been the sister of the bartender.

I saw she was fairly good looking. I thought I'd better really move in fast. Old Wrangler might just blow everything. I played the music and asked her to dance.

She stood a minute, looked at the bartender, shrugged her shoulders and said, "Why not?"

We danced and we danced. Then I'd set her down at the bar and we'd have another drink. I didn't let her out of reach. I could read that look on Wrangler's bulldog face too damn well.

Then I saw him heading for us. It was too late, he'd already set his mind on dancing with this little gal. I can't say as I blamed him. I reckon he figured this would be one last fling before he married. On the other hand he might not be thinking any such thing. He might just like her because she was a girl.

I thought fast. "Wrangler," I said, and it was the truth, "Myrna told me to be sure that you got a blood test today. She said it would ease her mind about the Rh Factor."

He stopped, blinking his little snake eyes, he said, "What's that?"

"Well, I don't exactly know, but she said it ran in her family, and it has something to do with having kids."

I'll be damned if it didn't work. He went back to the table and just stared.

A great big noise boomed outdoors. I jumped about three yards.

The bartender said, "It's raining."

It sure was. I could hear that water just splashing all over.

"Wrangler," I said, "you better take the pickup and run on in and see Dr. Price. That's who Myrna said was to give you the blood test."

"It's raining," he said, and just went on staring at a place on the side of the bar.

Finally I could see that Wrangler was afraid to go to the doctor so I walked up to a ragged-looking toothless old boy who was drinking the cheapest wine in the house. I asked him a question.

"Do you know where Dr. Price's office is?"

"Sure," he said. "I ain't never met him but the old lady goes there all the time fer her rheumatiz."

After a little explaining, two more drinks and a ten-dollar bill, he agreed to go to this Dr. Price and tell him his name was Wrangler Lewis and get a blood test.

Anything to please the new wife of my new boss.

I went back up and had another drink with the girl. Just in case his mind swung around to her again. Several people came in and all except one said, "It's raining." This one feller (he was about as big as me and Wrangler put together) came in, his arm swung around the shoulder of a half-pregnant woman. I'm sure they'd been celebrating something or other, for he said, "Who's raining?"

He had on a brand-new green shirt and she wore a loose flopping red dress. Where the rain had dropped off the shirt onto her dress there were green stripes. By god, she looked like a battle flag. They ordered muscatel wine, a sure sign of their condition whether they were drunk or not.

Wrangler was still staring at the bar, but this woman had filled up the spot he was hypnotized by. Pretty soon this big bastard with the big ears and big mouth noticed Wrangler staring. He walked over and said, "Hey, quit lookin' at my woman!"

Wrangler didn't even look up.

"I said, quit looking at my woman!" and he leaned over with his fists spread out on the table.

"What woman?" Wrangler asked.

"That'n," he said, pointing at the big-bellied red dress with the green stripes over the shoulders.

"I ain't staring at her," Wrangler said, scooting his chair around.

Now it makes no difference where you go in the world

there will always be one of these smart bastards to ruin a man's fun. But he might upset a lot more than that if he happened to land that wad of bone he used for a hand in the middle of Wrangler's face. We might have to postpone the wedding.

I got up, walked over and said, "Wrangler, this man is a head taller than you are, so I'm goin' to even things up."

I grabbed the son of a bitch around the neck and tried to pull his head off. It wouldn't come. I took another run across the room with him. I could see Wrangler was trying to help. He was pulling in the other direction. But one of the old boy's shoes came off and Wrangler fell backwards. Without this added weight we really began to move. The only thing that stopped us was a cement wall. I couldn't pull his head off and I couldn't drive it through the wall, so I just dropped him there and yelled, "Let's go."

On the way out, I could see the bartender calling the cops on the phone and I asked him, "Why didn't you stop that bastard from picking on my little friend? Then you wouldn't have to call the cops."

I didn't hear what he said because we stepped out into the rain. Our tough-necked friend failed to follow.

We jumped in the pickup, and I want to say that my lightning brains were still working. "Now, where will the police expect a couple of half-drunk cowboys to head?"

"Out of town," Wrangler said.

"*That* is right, so *up* town we're goin'!"

Thirteen

WE MANAGED to get uptown without having a wreck.

I even got the pickup parked fairly close to the curb. Wrangler wanted to head for another bar. I figured I ought to try to delay this.

"Listen, Wrangler, do you realize you ain't even bought Myrna a wedding present?"

"Never thought of it."

"Well now's the time. Come on, let's look around town here and see what we can find."

The rain had stopped and everybody was out on the sidewalk looking around. First we went in a store called a Five and Dime. I'll say this though, that sign was a big lie. The only thing in there for five cents was a package of chewing gum. We walked around looking at all those things: Bottles of everything on earth, hairpins, hairnets, hair spray, face powder, hand powder, and powder for other places, shoes, dishes, drawers for both men and girls.

They were pink, blue, yellow, red and all the colors in Myrna's flower garden. This brought something to mind.

"Wrangler, what does Myrna love more than anything on earth besides you?"

He kind of twisted his face around and said, "Them vegetable drinks." He acted so dang pleased with this that I hated to disappoint him.

"No, you're wrong. It's flowers."

"You're right," he said, getting the idea.

We walked over and bought a large, dun-colored flower-pot with a little baby lemon tree in it. They wrapped it all up and told Wrangler to be careful with it.

"I will," he said.

We barely left the store when he spotted another sa-loon. I knew I couldn't stop him from going in but maybe I could talk him into leaving soon. Seems like he was more shook up than ever before.

He downed three double shots while I coasted along on two singles. That brain of mine, that was getting so light-ning fast lately, started working again.

"You know, Wrangler, Myrna is goin' to ask us the first thing in the morning how we spent our day. Now wouldn't it be nice if we could say we spent it at the mov-ing pictures."

"All right that's what we'll tell her," he said motioning for another double shot.

"It ain't quite that easy." I said. "What if she asks what we saw?"

"That ain't no problem," he said, "the picture show's right around the corner."

"You ain't gettin' what I mean. What if she has seen this show herself and starts pumping us about it?"

"Oh."

"Drink up and let's go."

He gathered up his flowerpot easy-like and we walked around to the show. It had a big sign out front:

THE IRON SPIDER

A MONSTER DROPPED FROM OUTER SPACE TO

DEVOUR THE WORLD

I bought us a couple of tickets and we went in. They had a little old place that looked like a bar where they sold chewing gum, candy, soda pop and popcorn. I ordered us a bag of popcorn apiece, but when I handed it to Wrangler he said, "That ain't enough. I'm hungry." So he ordered two more bags.

I said, "How're you goin' to handle three bags of popcorn and that lemon tree?"

He didn't answer. He just took off his hat and emptied all the popcorn in it. We went to the show.

It was hard to see in there and we both had the blind staggers. A little feller carrying a flashlight without any light in it, took us down in the middle of the place and we finally got settled.

The show was just starting. A great big flat-looking thing was flying over the top of the world. Inside it was a bunch of green men who had a face in front and the same face in back. Their feet were the same way. They reminded me of some of those little peanut cars you see around these big towns. I watched and I watched but there wasn't any way to tell the front from the back. I kept thinking that maybe if one of their women would show up a feller might get a clue.

All of a sudden a lot of loud, scary music started playing (I never did see where the band was but it played during the whole show) and a great big iron spider dropped out of that flying machine. It came down on a thread like any spider would except it was about seven jillion times bigger. On the ends of its iron legs were some bucket-looking things. Soon as it landed it started sticking out those iron legs and sucking everything right up into that big belly. It was sure enough boogery.

Then the scene changed to a wad of scientific fellers talking to the army, and one of the army fellers wasn't no feller at all, it was a woman who looked a little like Lolane. They were calling out army tanks, and thousands of soldiers and airplanes by the hundred. But this spider just went right on through this city knocking over buildings as big as mountains, swatting airplanes out of the sky like sick mosquitoes, and sucking people up those iron legs as fast as he got to them. One of those science fellers said that human food was like fuel to this monster. He really had plenty, looked like to me.

Wrangler was chewing popcorn so hard and fast that folks all around were turning to us and saying, "Shhhhh." They gave us dirty looks too.

After a while that spider took in after a handsome soldier and this pretty woman. He stuck out one of those iron legs and slowly but surely that poor woman was pulled right up into that bucket.

It was too much for Wrangler. He jumped up and yelled, "Kill the mean son of a bitch!" Popcorn went everywhere. People got all upset, and the little man with the flashlight came down and told us to be quiet or leave. I finally got Wrangler settled enough to watch the picture.

The woman was completely gone and the soldier was fighting like hell trying to hang on to the edge of the iron leg. Then all of a sudden the spider sort of fell backwards trembling and began to weave and sink lower and lower. Finally he fell over, kicked a time or two and died. It sure was a relief.

I was really surprised at how smart that soldier was. Come to find out that wasn't a real woman at all — just a dummy made of wax. The wax choked that spider to death and thereby the world was saved.

Wrangler just sat there pumping his lungs after the show was over.

We finally got enough strength to get outside. I expected it to be dark but the sun was still two hours high. Wrangler didn't say a word. He was shaking all over and his eyes were kind of glazed like melted glass. He could see good enough though to read a sign that said HARRY'S SALOON.

He commenced pouring those drinks down and the most I could get out of him was his usual grunt. This didn't look good. The more he drank the more I could tell that spider was on his mind. I played the jukebox, and told all sorts of lies trying to get his mind off the show. Nothing worked.

After a while I said, "Let's go to another saloon."

He got up and followed me out. We walked down the street without talking. I was hoping I could get him to the pickup and haul him back to the Inn. Then I figured I'd get him in the room with a full bottle and just let him forget all these things that seemed to be on his back.

Well we passed a doorway and on the window next to it was a sign that said:

BETTY'S BEAUTY
SALON

Now Wrangler's not very tall when he's stepping his highest, and I reckon the only word he saw was the bottom one. He just automatically turned in. I followed.

There sat eight ladies under eight hair dryers. Some were cleaning their fingernails, others were reading.

Old Wrangler stiffened like a frozen post. Then he hauled off and threw his flowerpot at one of the hair dryers. His aim was good. The dryer banged, the pot broke and the dirt and the lemon tree all came down on top of the woman's fresh-washed head.

Then with a wild yell he attacked one of the dryers. The women jumped all directions, overturning things. The ones who didn't faint ran out in the street screaming "Police! Police! Madman!"

Wrangler didn't seem to notice anything like this. He had one of the hair dryers down choking hell out of it and when that didn't seem to make any difference he began to beat it against the floor.

He was yelling, "Don't worry ladies, I'll kill this god-damned iron spider!"

Well, he killed several before the police got there. I just stood and watched. I'd already given up. It was just too much for old tired Dusty.

The police grabbed him and I said, "Here now, this man's a hero. He's drunk and he thought those dryers were spider legs."

With that they just loaded me up and took me along with the hero. Right in jail they threw us and locked the thick iron door. Now an old uncle of mine (the one that wasn't a preacher) once told me that if you were on a party and didn't get in jail, you hadn't had any fun. This was one time he was wrong. What really got me was that before I could chew Wrangler's tail out, the little ugly bastard had gone to sleep.

There ain't no use whatever in telling all about the night. It was long.

The next morning after one of those sorry jail breakfasts, we went before the judge. I tried like hell to remember the vice-president's name who'd offered his help at Myrna's party. I just couldn't think straight all of a sudden. Then I thought about calling Myrna and realized that my lightning brain was slipping a little there, too. If she didn't find out about this we'd have old Wrangler hitched today and then it would be too late. Yes, sir, today was the day.

Well, the judge let us know right off that he was God and owned the world and could do anything he wanted to with us. I agreed with everything he said. I'd learned long ago that there's no justice with judges. Especially if you talk back.

He then proceeded to fine us the limit, for drunkenness, disturbing the peace, fighting and destroying several inanimate objects. Namely hair dryers. Then on top of that we had to pay for those hair dryers. Our rate of payment was based on the price of brand-new ones, even though they were several years old. We paid. The price for being a hero really comes high these days.

I was glad to get out of there even though we only had six dollars and eighty-four cents left out of all our pay, all Myrna's fifty-dollar bills and all that money the Englishman had given us. It was a damn good thing it was the day of the great wedding.

Fourteen

I'll say one thing, *that* Myrna doesn't do *any*thing half-way. People were driving up in Cadillacs and RR cars from just about everywhere.

Out by the swimming pool three cooks wearing great tall white hats were barbecuing a whole beef. They kept turning him over the coals and on a windy day you could have smelled it as far as Hi Lo. It made a feller's taster act up. Four or five waiters were running around with their hands turned upside down carrying trays of vegetable drinks.

It was sunshiny and the wind was still. People were seated all around the swimming pool, talking and drinking and waiting. Every little bit a car would drive up and unload an armload of flowers. It made me kind of sad that our lemon tree hadn't survived the picture show.

Old Fooler was standing with his head up over the corral looking wild-eyed. He was getting fat and mean.

Myrna called me into the house to try to help Wrangler get ready. It sure was a job mashing him into that tuxedo. In fact, we never did get him in it completely.

The phone kept ringing and Myrna would answer, "Oh, I'm so sorry you couldn't make it, dear. Well, thank you, dear. How are things in New York? Tell Joe 'Hello' for me, darling. Oh yes, he's a sweetie pie. We'll be so happy. Yes, dear, we'll see you in Mexico in January. I will. I will. Bye now."

It just kept on — one thing after another. Then the preacher came in and made a big show out of what was going to take place. It seems we missed some kind of rehearsal.

Myrna's personal maid loped in with the daily paper all spread out and her finger pointing to a certain spot on the front page. I got the cold feeling a baby mouse must get when he's just been swallered by a rattlesnake.

Myrna said, "Not now, Celia, I can't read now. What is it that's so important?"

I made several signs at the maid but she smiled back exactly like Old Fooler after he's kicked you in the belly.

"Madam," she said, "it's *very* important."

Myrna stopped what she was doing and said, "All right, I don't suppose a minute longer will hurt, will it, honey pie?"

Old Wrangler grinned back kind of silly-like, "I reckon not, Myrna baby."

I had already read over her shoulder all I wanted to see and that was this:

HEIRESS' BRIDEGROOM SPENDS PRE-WEDDING
NIGHT IN JAIL

Myrna turned white even through that suntanned
makeup. She glared at Wrangler and spit out, "The cin-
ema my foot!"

Before Myrna could say more, the maid handed her the
phone, halfway shouting with excitement, "It's Dr. Price.
He says its extremely urgent."

Myrna took the phone. She was shaking so hard it rattled against her golden earrings.

"What? An alcoholic? And it showed positive on . . .
on . . . !" and right there words failed her. Whatever
was positive must've really been bad. She dropped the
phone right across Wrangler's head, screaming, "You
filthy beast, you've given me that horrible disease." Then
she threw the mirror, and a big bottle of lotion. She
tried to throw the dressing table. Then she just stopped
and screamed and pulled her hair. "You beast, you vile
beast!"

I gathered up the little beast's boots, levis and his shirt.
He grabbed his hat and we retreated. I will say this,
Myrna's screams had only interested the guests. I heard
one of them say as we broke out of the house, "Seems the
groom is taking advantage of his marriage privileges
somewhat early." But when they saw the groom bare-
footed with a big, old, greasy cowboy hat on and his little
potbelly hanging out over those shiny black britches, a
lot of voices stilled, but not Myrna's. We could still hear
her screaming.

"Listen," I said, thinking lightning fast, "she'll calm down in a minute and you'll just have to tell her the truth. That we sent somebody else in your place. That wasn't *your* POSITIVE blood at all."

Wrangler just stood there shaking. He had a ten-day hangover to help him, but I believe his courage would have snapped anyway.

She was at an open window now still pulling her hair and yelling. For a minute she kind of choked down. That's when we heard the music.

Around the big circle driveway came a truck — a large truck — and it was hauling a whole band. As it came on around the circle, the driver started squeezing the horn and a man was beating a drum like he was trying to kill it. Every man on that truck started blowing or beating something.

I heard a loud crashing noise down towards the stables and saw Old Fooler booger and jump right through the corral. He was plumb wild and didn't know where to go. He ran this way and that but there was always some wedding guests in his way. Finally I reckon he must've spotted me and Wrangler because he came tearing around the swimming pool scattering people everywhere. He ran right up beside us. He was shaking as bad as Myrna.

Suddenly he kind of settled down and went to gobbling some prize-winning dahlias out of the flower bed, raising his head, snorting and shaking dirt off the roots every time he got another mouthful. Then he did it. There wasn't any hope now. It was all done. I don't really think Old Fooler meant it as an insult. I just think he was plain scared into it at the sight of all this society. He lifted his tail and took a big dump right out on the patio with a pure white flower hanging out each side of his mouth.

There is not another thing to tell about old Wrangler's wedding day except this — we left.

Fifteen

Now six dollars and eighty-four cents is lots of money
if you're well fed and know where you can get another
meal. But it ain't much in four days without either. As
soon as the word got to the Inn they kicked us right out.
We moved to the edge of town, slept in our bedrolls
and ate cheese and crackers every day like it was pure
honey.

We went into town and started asking around for a
ranch job. Seemed like everybody was well supplied.

One feller asked me why we didn't draw welfare pay-
ments. I didn't exactly understand what it was and I
knew less after I talked to the Welfare people. We were
offered a job in a filling station, but we didn't even have
a social security card. I tried to find that vice-president
to borrow one of his. He must have been out of town.

Finally we went to an employment agency. The man
said, "Tomorrow's Friday. We have a client coming in

who needs a couple of cowboys to break out a string of broncs. Will that be all right?"

I said, "Listen, as hungry as we are, I'll fight six wild tigers barehanded if you'll let me eat the remains."

"All right then, be here at two o'clock tomorrow afternoon and we'll see what we can do."

It was a long time till then. That night I tried to eat some of Old Fooler's oats. It wasn't that he was stingy. It was just that I couldn't get them down with him looking at me.

Wrangler said, "You've heard that song, ain't you, about the hobo who was so hungry he could eat grass. Well, I'm so empty I could eat the ground it grows in."

"This here ground's too full of rocks."

"Yeah," he said, "I done tried it."

Two o'clock finally did come. It took all the strength we had left to climb the stairs up to the second story. We went in and sat down. At two-thirty this rancher still hadn't showed. I was too weak to ask the smiling secretary if something had gone wrong. In fact, I could only smile back at her with one side of my mouth.

Right about three o'clock the man who ran the office walked in with the rancher.

That is right! It was Jim Ed Love!

Weak as he was, Wrangler jumped and ran to the window. The only thing that stopped him from jumping out was the fact he got tangled up in a bunch of those venetian blinds.

I dragged him away from the window saying, "It wouldn't do you no good to jump, Wrangler. We ain't but two stories up. All you'd do is break a bunch of bones."

He stopped kicking. We both looked at Jim Ed. He smiled and stuck his belly out over his fancy silver and turquoise belt buckle.

"You boys look like you've had a fine time. A *fine* time."

We just stood and swallered air.

"How about us going down the street here and getting a great big juicy sirloin steak with potatoes and hot gravy to boot?" Jim Ed said.

Us two ex-city slickers just followed him down the stairs rubbing our growling bellies and licking our lips.